BELLE HARBOR
COZY MYSTERIES
COLLECTION

BOOKS 1 - 3: A COZY CULINARY MYSTERY

SUE HOLLOWELL

CONTENTS

CUPCAKES AND CATASTROPHE

A Belle Harbor Cozy Mystery

Book 1

CHAPTER ONE

"**U**ncle Jack, you don't have to do that. Why don't you sit and rest a bit?" My dear uncle had been working nonstop ever since I had agreed to move to Belle Harbor. I wasn't so sure about the arrangement, but I was ready for a big change in my life. And I couldn't get a much bigger change than leaving the cold East Coast city of Boston, Massachusetts, and leaping across the country to the small, sunny beach town of Belle Harbor. In some ways, it was an easy transition. Who could argue with the weather? And Uncle Jack was one of my favorite people on the planet. The scariest part was finally pursuing my dream of opening a bakery, just like my Grandma Luna had done.

"Don't be silly, Tilly," Uncle Jack said. "Hey, I made a rhyme."

I rolled my eyes. Truthfully, Uncle Jack's organization system left a lot to be desired. He ran the Checkered Past Antique shop right on the boardwalk at Belle Harbor. I couldn't see how he had an inkling of what was in the store. From my vantage point, it was a hodgepodge of junk. A set of six crystal wine glasses sat next to a statue of an old sea mariner holding binoculars, next to a two-foot-tall silver-stemmed bowl holding what looked like fake dill pickles. Somehow, he and his brother had made it work for decades.

"I can't thank you enough, Unkie. You really are making my dream come true." I strolled through the aisles of treasures, surveying how I might help him better arrange the pieces for sale. I made mental notes, not wanting to upset the apple cart on my first official day. I stopped and observed him furiously working in the corner he had cleared out to make room for my very first bakeshop. Moving items out of the space for my supplies created even bigger piles of antiques. "You really should let me help you."

He lifted his head from his focus at the work counter he had set up for my baking. "Oh, Til." His voiced cracked. He stepped toward me and held out his hand. "I would do anything for you."

Somehow, he had gotten a smudge of flour on his face. I reached up and wiped it away. He tilted his head and smiled warmly. We both returned to the baking corner. He had fully equipped me with a little kitchen to begin my new life as a baker. The area had an oven, sink, cabinets, and counters for supplies and tools. The only thing was... his system for setting it up looked exactly the same as his antique store. I would later find a way to hopefully, without his noticing, shift things around to be more usable for my purposes.

"OK, let's sit for a bit," he said. I followed him to the side of the cash register, where we each plopped into an Elizabethan-style wooden chair. I felt like we were waiting for the jester to arrive and perform for us. Uncle Jack was a spry seventy-year-old man with vigor for life. I knew my move here would inject all kinds of adventure into my life. I just wasn't sure what it would be. He had lost a bit of his step ever since his brother, and partner in the store, had passed away. Those two together caused a lot of mischief, according to my mom. But I had only ever seen them as a hoot while I was growing up.

Mom and Dad never knew what to do with me, so they shipped me off every summer to stay with Jack and Frank. Little did they know, it only emboldened my creative side. I was about as far as you could get from the stodgy professions of my parents.

I looked at him and reached over to grab his hand. It was well worn from a life of physical labor. My uncle was never one to shy away from hard work. His balding head and trim white beard framed his warm brown eyes. That man really would do anything for his friends and family.

"I'm thinking I'll name the bakery Luna's Bakeshop. What do you think?"

He rested his head against the tall back of the chair, closed his eyes, and smiled. "She would be so pleased you're following in her footsteps." Grandma Luna was as much of a kook as my uncles. I couldn't figure out how in a million years my mom turned out the way she did. Perhaps a reverse rebellion from a wild and crazy mother of her own. He turned and looked at me. "You look like her too. In her day, she wouldn't have dyed her hair blue like you have. But everything else? The spitting image."

That couldn't have been a higher compliment. I would take that as a sign I was on the right track for my new life. "So I'm planning to make Grandma's signature cream-filled cupcakes for my inaugural recipe."

Uncle Jack shook his head. "Tilly, you're going to be a hit in this town. They'll be lining up out the door. And I don't mean just customers."

I stood, turned, and pointed a finger at him. "Don't you dare fix me up. I just got out of a relationship, and I'm nowhere near ready for another. I'm going to focus on building my business and just enjoying myself for a change." I moved to a nearby table, piled high with antiques, and shifted a few things around to busy myself. Truthfully, I wanted to hide from life in my bakery. The ink hadn't even dried on my divorce papers. Any thoughts of that life, three thousand miles away, hurt my heart. And if I let my mind go there, it quickly became a downward spiral. In time I would process it. But not today.

Uncle Jack pushed himself out of the chair. I heard a couple of cracks in the quiet store, probably both from his knees and the old furniture. He steadied himself and said, "Let's step outside and see what's going on with the kite festival. I could use some warmth in these old bones."

I looked around. "But who's going to watch the store?"

He waved his arm around the space. "Everyone's at the kite festival. And besides, we'll only go far enough so that we can still see if someone comes in."

That was something else I would have to get used to. In the big city, if you left your business unattended, you would certainly come back to looters. OK, maybe not that bad, but why take a chance?

We stepped through the doorway to the bright sun and warmth. I stopped, closed my eyes, and lifted my face, taking in a deep breath. I could easily get used to this weather.

With my move to the beach, I had needed to get a whole new wardrobe. I took pleasure in donating my winter woolies and buying some things that more closely fit my personality. No more prim and proper styles; now I was all into preppy, casual, beach fun.

Along with getting my bobbed hair colored to match the ocean, I purchased several pairs of Converse shoes in just about every color and style to match a mood. Today's pair matched the blues and greens of the sea. Of course, I stocked up on T-shirts, and as Grandma Luna would call them, pedal pushers. In modern lingo, capris. Stepping into that outfit this morning and doing a once-over in the full-length mirror made me feel like I was one step further along my journey to a new life. And to spend time with Uncle Jack, who I expected to be my partner-in-crime was a dream come true.

CHAPTER TWO

"Why don't we just sit here so we can stay close in case someone wants to buy something?" I gestured to the bench up against the outer wall of the antique shop. I wasn't convinced it was safe to venture very far. Though, if someone did steal something, it might just make a bit more room to organize what remained.

Uncle Jack turned to look at me. "Tilly, don't be a worry wart. I've been doing this a long time. It'll be fine. Live a little, darlin'." He strolled out toward the beach.

I looked both ways, didn't see any sketchy characters, and followed his path. I crossed the boardwalk that separated our shops from the greater part of the beach. The official portion of the kite competition was on a break. Amateurs attempted to hoist their kites into the air.

I stopped again, breathed in deep, and gazed up and down the beach. Kites of all styles were in flight. I jogged to catch up with my uncle. Beach living must have provided him ample opportunity to keep in shape. By the time I reached him, I had to stop and catch my breath. "Uncle Jack," I said, bent over, wheezing.

He turned and came back to my side. "Oh, girl. Soon you'll have the stamina of a seventy-year-old." He rocked his head back in laughter. "Isn't this beautiful?" He swept his arm around. I wasn't sure what he referred to, but everything as far as I could see was indeed breathtaking. The blue-green ocean sparkled with the sun glinting off the water. The warmth permeated to my bones, like a blanket hugging me. Kids squealed, enjoying family time in their little huddles up and down the beach while watching the kite competition.

I stood and held out my hand to him. "This is amazing. What a fun event."

Even though I had lived in Boston, which had access to multiple beaches, neither my parents nor my ex had any interest in visiting and enjoying the ocean. It was all work and no play. When I did have a moment to myself, I made a beeline to the coast. It refreshed my soul like nothing else. The expanse of the water, sky, and sand gave me peace. It fueled my creativity—the little time I had to spend on it. My bookkeeping job helped pay the bills, but it did nothing to serve my passion. I longed to follow in Grandma Luna's footsteps and own my own bakery. I had to pinch myself to make sure my current reality wasn't a dream.

I didn't have much time with her, but when Grandma Luna and I were together, I felt like we were kindred spirits. My parents referred to her derisively as a hippie that never grew up. Whatever she was, she always seemed incredibly joyful with life. I desperately longed for that. It wasn't until after a lot of conversations that finally my ex agreed to culinary school. I remember the day vividly. A huge rock in my throat almost kept me from speaking my mind. I had visited Grandma in the hospital as she lay dying. Her body was wearing out. She took my hand, looked deeply into my eyes, and urged me to follow my passion. She had squeezed my hand for emphasis, and at that moment some sort of boldness overcame me like never before.

With my borrowed confidence from my grandma, I told my ex I would be attending culinary school. He blinked and took a step back. I stood with my hands on my hips like Wonder Woman, not willing to budge an inch. This was happening. I had no way of knowing it would also lead to the end of my marriage.

I had gathered my breath sufficiently to continue walking along the beach.

"This is day two. Every year there's a handful of the most competitive fliers who duke it out. Looks like the perennial favorite is in third place." Uncle Jack gestured to a leader board that listed last names in rank order. At the top was Burkhart followed by Simon, then Powell. "That's not going to sit well with Maverick. I know he's been tuning up his gear for quite some time. He doesn't like to lose."

I shaded my eyes and looked at Uncle Jack. "You know him?"

"Oh, yeah. I know most everyone in town." We continued roaming around the sand.

I stopped. "Don't you think we should return to the store?" I turned to look back and could barely see the door of the antique shop. It didn't appear anyone was near, so maybe he was right. We were safe for a short period of time.

"OK. If it'll make you feel better, big-city girl." He chuckled. "I'm hopeful you'll shed your stress and join me in chill town."

"Me too," I said. We retraced our steps back to the store. "Uncle Jack, can you slow down just a bit?" I stopped. How was that man so fit?

He came back to where I stood. "It's settled. I'm going to buy you a moped. You'll need that anyway when you start delivering all of your wares."

I shook my head and resumed walking, trying to set the pace. "You don't have to do that."

He jetted out front of me, and I did my best to keep up. At this rate, I would need a nap when we got back. "I insist. Plus, I know the gal who runs the shop. She'll give me a good deal."

I attempted to half-jog, hoping I wouldn't collapse right there and end my new life just as it was getting started. "Well, I'll pay you back. Every penny. I counted on other people my entire life. And now I'm counting on myself."

Uncle Jack abruptly stopped and pointed a finger at me. "I don't want to hear any more of that talk, missy. You are an incredible woman. We each take our own path. You've learned a lot that you can now apply to this new season. But it wasn't for naught."

He was right. My journey brought me to this point, so it couldn't have been all bad. And I had my very own amateur therapist to keep me grounded. What an incredible first day on my new odyssey. I looked forward to getting back to my little corner kitchen and starting on those cupcakes.

I could easily see the door to the shop now and my anxiety decreased a bit. I only hoped we weren't ripped off during our little jaunt down the beach.

Uncle Jack turned to me and said, "See? Everything's fine." He grinned and displayed those hard-earned laugh lines. I smiled. Eventually I would adjust. How could you not?

We both whipped our heads around as a blood-curdling scream emanated from the direction of the shop. Maybe I spoke too soon? Like a man fifty years his junior, my uncle sped off toward the horrific sound. I followed as closely as possible but was unable to keep up. As we got closer, it became clear the shriek was from the vacant shop next to Checkered Past Antiques. We both entered through the propped-open door.

Standing about six feet inside with her hand over her mouth was an elderly woman. Her eyes were as large as plates. Uncle Jack and I both followed her gaze to see a dead body on the floor in the middle of the room. She shook her head, unable to speak.

Uncle Jack took a step closer, and I grabbed his arm. He turned and said, "That's Cal. One of the kite competition judges. He's been strangled."

CHAPTER THREE

A whimper came from the woman to our side. I judged her to be about the same age as my uncle. She looked like she was attending a formal tea party. A string of pearls topped her floral, sleeveless dress. A small straw hat covered her pixie silver haircut. A bold, dark set of eyeglasses sat atop her nose. She lowered her chin and peered over the top of the glasses.

"Why is he here?" She pointed at the body, averting her eyes. "This is my building."

Uncle Jack and I looked at each other and shrugged. "The kite competition judges were using this space. I didn't know anyone owned this," Uncle Jack said.

The lady stepped away from the body and angled herself toward the door. With her hand shielding her eyes, she said, "You need to get him out of here." She took two more steps toward the door, her heels clopping loudly throughout the empty room.

I peeked at the body and saw a man younger than Uncle Jack laying on his side like he was taking a nap. The table where the judges sat to perform the scoring was on its side. The three metal folding chairs were haphazardly strewn away from the table, like someone had scooted them out before turning the table over.

The man wore board shorts, flip flops, and a black- and white-striped referee shirt. The scoring pages were strewn across the floor. The easel and chart paper with scores lay on its side. The list and order of names mirrored those on the chart at the beach. Who would do this? I imagined the competition was serious, but enough to take out a judge who didn't score your way?

A sound came from the woman's bag that was awfully familiar. Maybe the loud voices coming in from outside were playing with my brain. Again I heard it, distinctly sounding like a cat. A tiny paw reached out from under her hand. The woman was apparently shielding its eyes from the scene. "Oh, Princess Guinevere. It will be OK. Mommy will get you out of here soon and away from the bad man." The woman took another step away, almost to the door. "Please take care of this mess. I can't believe this is happening. Maybe I'll have to reconsider opening my bookstore here after all."

Uncle Jack looked at Cal and stepped between him and this lady. He tilted his head, bushy brows furrowed. "And who are you?"

The woman huffed, her hand still trying to cover the squirming cat. "Well, I'm Florence Kennedy, of course. Of the famous Kennedys."

Uncle Jack glanced at me and back at the woman. "Well, Flo, that doesn't answer my question."

The woman straightened up and stepped toward Uncle Jack. "That's Florence. And I bought this building. I came by to see it before I have everything moved in. I didn't know anyone would be here. Let alone a dead person." She flicked her arm around Uncle Jack toward Cal, then shivered like she was cold. Another meow from Florence's purse caused us all to look at her cat. "And Princess Guinevere is so upset. I don't know if she will ever be the same again after seeing that." Again, she gestured toward Cal.

"Cats are resilient. She'll be fine. Why don't we go outside so we can talk?" A much louder meow came from the opposite side of the room. We all turned our heads and saw a black cat with white paws and a white chest strutting past Cal's body. "Oh, look. It's Willie," Uncle Jack said.

As Willie strolled past Cal, he took the opportunity to grab what must have been a piece of kite string and began playing with it. "Oh no," I said. "We should probably get him out of here so he doesn't mess with the crime scene." I took a step toward Willie and crouched. "Here, kitty, kitty."

Willie stopped batting the string for a moment and took a step in my direction. He quickly halted and resumed his play.

Uncle Jack said, "Let me try. He knows me. C'mon Willie. Let's get back home." He scooped Willie into his arm, getting a better look at Cal. "You're right, Tilly. That string looks like it may have been the murder weapon. It's wrapped around Cal's neck. I think it's kite string."

Florence gasped. "I had no idea this part of town was so rough. Why didn't the realtor tell me it was running rampant with hoodlums?" Princess Guinevere struggled to get her head out from under Florence's hand. Willie also began to seriously wiggle out of Uncle Jack's arms.

"We should probably get these two out of here before we end up like a scratching post. Florence, why don't you come next door to Checkered Past Antiques while we wait for the police?" Uncle Jack offered.

"Do you own that junk store?" she asked.

Uncle Jack's cheeks drooped and he frowned. That statement was a dagger to the heart. The store was his and his brother Frank's pride and joy. "I'll have you know, Flo, we have a lot of precious and high-end items. People travel from all over to come see us." Uncle Jack hugged Willie to his chest and stomped out of the building to the sidewalk.

I stepped to Uncle Jack's side and put my hand on his arm. "Is Willie your cat?"

He closed his eyes and shook his head. "No. He belongs to Justin who rents the apartment upstairs from the antique store." He tilted his head down the sidewalk toward Checkered Past Antiques. He turned to see if Florence was following him and entered his store. Uncle Jack put Willie on the floor and he took off like a rocket, taking shelter behind the display counter.

Florence stepped just barely inside and scanned the room, looking like she might reconsider Uncle Jack's offer.

"I'm going to call the police. You're welcome to take a seat while we wait," Uncle Jack said and gestured to a couple of chairs matching those on the outside of the store.

Looking down at her cat and pausing, Florence slowly made her way to the seat. She wiped her gloved hand across the fabric, removing any invisible dust and looking at her fingers. She made eye contact with Uncle Jack, shook her head, and sat on the edge of the chair. Princess Guinevere poked her head out of the bag with a huge sneeze. Florence gasped and put her hand over the cat's head again.

Willie peeked around the corner toward the sound he heard and looked at me. I shrugged. He looked at Princess Guinevere again and tiptoed a couple of steps toward her, wisely wary of the duo, who seemed completely out of place. I suspected after all of this drama, the deal for the purchase of the building next door would be null and void.

I didn't feel a need to engage Florence in conversation. This might be the last time we would see her. I heard Uncle Jack on the phone to the police, reporting our find. I was sure it wouldn't be long before someone would arrive to take our statements and gather clues from the scene. I hoped it would be soon. I was itching to get busy on my debut baking voyage. I could almost taste the cream that was part of Grandma Luna's legendary cupcakes. Thankfully, I now lived in a place that made it easier to get outside and be active. Tasting my treats would test my waistline. I sighed. I wanted more adventure in this new phase of my life. But finding dead bodies was not what I envisioned.

CHAPTER FOUR

"**G**ood morning, Uncle Jack." I was so excited for my first day of baking I couldn't sleep the night before. "Where can I get some of that coffee?" I wove my way through the stacks of aisles teeming with merchandise. I held my breath, almost afraid of disturbing something and creating an avalanche.

"C'mon back. I've always got a pot going." He got a cup from the shelf and poured it full of the steaming elixir.

I took it, inhaled the aroma, and took a sip. I coughed. "Wow, that's strong stuff."

"I figured we would need it today. That was quite the first day you had yesterday." He took his coffee and sat in one of the chairs bordering the small table. He pointed at the other chair for me to sit. "Take a load off before we get too busy for our day."

I could learn a thing or two from my Uncle Jack about priorities and not stressing. He was as cool as a cucumber yesterday when that dead body appeared. Thankfully, due to his calm state I didn't freak out. At least on the outside. I was sure my restless night was also prompted by the mystery we had on our hands—and a murderer we had in our midst.

I sat and gripped the coffee cup with both hands, tipping and gulping half of it down. I felt an almost instant jolt from the caffeine. I looked at my uncle, slouched in his chair, gazing into the distance. He slowly turned and said, "I hope you don't let the events of yesterday scare you off. It really is safe here. Though, you probably had more of that to worry about in the big city."

I smiled. I didn't want to worry him. But I was scared. We certainly had a higher crime rate where I moved from, but never in my life had I seen a murdered body. "I'm OK. Your friend Barney was very gentle in his questioning yesterday. I think he even handled Florence well."

Barney Houston was the police chief of Belle Harbor. He probably dealt more with drunk and rowdy beach-goers than he did with dead bodies in this small town. But he acted like this was the millionth time he was investigating a murder.

I shivered at the thought of Cal laying on the floor, envisioning someone strangling him with kite string right next door. Did it happen when we were in the building? Or when we were on our walk? I racked my brain to remember anyone I happened to see near the antique store.

"Yeah, he's a pro. Barney and I go way back. He's been visiting more now that Frank has passed. He doesn't think I know what he's up to." Uncle Jack bowed his head, sat on the edge of his chair, and sighed. "Truth be told, I'm glad to see him. It has been lonely without my brother. I can't actually remember a time when Frank and I weren't together." His voice got quiet.

I scooted to the edge of my chair and got up to refill my cup. "I'm glad he's here for you."

Uncle Jack stood. "I do have a great friend group. That reminds me. We've got our weekly poker game Friday. Normally I'd close the store a bit early. But if you wouldn't mind?" He raised those bushy eyebrows toward me. How could I resist those—and this kind, gentle, supportive man?

"Of course I'll watch the shop for you, Unkie," I said.

He held out his hand to halt me pouring any more coffee. "Hold off on that a bit. I have a surprise for you." He put his empty cup on the table, grabbed my hand, and led me from the store. I was not one for surprises. I preferred having control of things in my life. For many years, I went along to get along. But that always felt like my life wasn't my own. I tried to organize and arrange what I could, but it was never enough. I was finally getting some clarity about my future that gave me peace. But with the Uncle Jack factor, I might just have to learn how to be more spontaneous.

We emerged onto the sidewalk along the beachfront shops. He guided me in the opposite direction than we had ventured yesterday. I couldn't fathom what he had in store for me. At this early hour, a few people were out and about. Mostly joggers on the boardwalk and a few families staking out their space on the beach for another day of the kite festival.

"Where are we going?" I looked over my shoulder at the antique shop. How in the world did he do so well in business when he frequently left the place unattended?

"Well, I figured you needed a better way to get around town to deliver your bakery items." He continued his brisk pace, causing me to start wheezing as I struggled to keep up.

"You're way ahead of me. I don't have any deliveries planned for a while. I was just going to sell the items from the antique shop," I said, gasping in between sentences.

Uncle Jack stopped. I suspected he realized he was running me ragged but didn't mention it. "Girl, you've got to be thinking big. You should go into Mocha Joe's and set up an arrangement with him to supply pastries. It would be a match made in heaven." He winked. Was he already setting me up for more than a business relationship? My stomach gurgled at the thought.

I slowed my pace and he matched my steps. "That's a good idea. I'll put it on my list to check out," I said. My breath finally steadied.

"Here we are," he said and turned into a Nelson's Moped Rental Shop. He grinned from ear to ear. "This will be perfect for you to get around town. We can get you one which has a basket to hold your deliveries."

"It's really too much. I can't," I said.

"Nonsense. I insist. Frank left money for me. And this is what I want to do. Hi Anna." Uncle Jack headed to the counter.

The woman waved. "Hi Jack. I'm all ready for you." Her long blonde hair bobbed behind her in a ponytail as she walked toward us. She pointed to the door of the shop.

"Beautiful Anna. This is my niece Tilly that I told you about."

Anna stuck her hand out and we shook. "Nice to meet you," I said and swung around and glared at Uncle Jack, my eyes wide.

"It's settled, I'm doing this for you." He led us outside to a row of three mopeds lined up against the front wall. Anna and I followed.

I stood with my hands on my hips, attempting to strike a pose of confidence. I had never ridden a moped. And my bicycle skills were quite rusty too. "I wouldn't know how to ride one."

Uncle Jack looked at Anna, and she handed him a key. "I'll show you. Easy peasy." He stepped up to the first moped in the row and swung his leg over it. He inserted the key and put on the helmet, pulling the strap snugly over his bushy beard. That man was bold.

I quickly stepped to his side and whispered, "Uncle Jack, what about your glaucoma?" I peeked at Anna. Did she not know that his eyesight wasn't the best? I had to stop this disaster waiting to happen.

"It's fine," he said.

I didn't know how it could be fine. "Why doesn't Anna show me?" I looked at her for support in my pleas.

"Tilly." He called me over and tipped his head in a conspiratorial manner, looking over my shoulder at Anna. He said, "Justin hooked me up with some marijuana. It's really helped." He sat tall. "Just watch." I hoped I wasn't about to see the end of my uncle. He started the moped and sped off down the sidewalk, out to the boardwalk.

My heart raced and I shook my head. Anna stepped up next to me. "He thinks his glaucoma 'treatment,'"—she used air quotes—"is illegal. We keep telling him that it's legal now to have marijuana. But I think he likes believing he's doing something nefarious. It really does seem to help his eyesight."

I took a deep breath and watched my uncle speed along the boardwalk, earning him a few dirty looks from the early morning beach crowd. At that moment, I had no doubt the universe had put him and I together at this point in time—just what we both needed in our lives.

I talked Uncle Jack into riding the moped back to the antique store until I could get more practice driving it. That might have been against my better judgment as he whizzed past me and several people, one hand waving in the air, yelling 'yeehaw.' I closed my eyes and gulped, saying a silent prayer that he would return in one piece. It was no wonder he was a free spirit as the son of Grandma Luna, who always danced to her own music. The sun had now risen, beginning to warm up the growing crowd on the beach.

The colorful Ferris wheel was now running with a long line of people waiting for their ride. The rhythmic sound of the waves coming to shore slowed my heartrate. I inhaled the salt air. The ambiance in Belle Harbor was something I could easily get used to. A feeling of freedom, a permanent vacation, and a whole new life lay before me.

My goal was to focus on becoming the best baker I could. The temporary spot Uncle Jack had created in the Checkered Past Antiques' store would do until I established my business. I looked ahead and saw

Unkie had parked the moped and returned to the store. I couldn't wait to see what life had in store for me. It had to be better than up 'til now. This was going to be a great day.

CHAPTER FIVE

No doubt the sea air and the excitement of the last couple of days exhausted me for a good night's sleep. The sun was up, and I felt like I was already behind for my day. Bakers started their shifts by 4:00 a.m., and it was several hours after that. I just couldn't bring myself to ride my new moped yet, so I walked the few blocks from my little rental cottage to the antique store. I rounded the corner to the sidewalk along the beachfront shops and saw the Checkered Past Antiques' door propped open and ready for business. Light blazed through the front window, illuminating the bench in front of the store.

I entered the shop and didn't see a soul. Two deep voices came from the table and chairs in the corner that Uncle Jack had set up for his coffee chats. I teased him that it was his good ole boys club.

"Over here, Tilly," came Uncle Jack's voice as I saw fingers wiggling in the air. The smell of coffee started my taste buds salivating. I needed a jolt of java to get my day going.

"Hi guys," I said, reaching for the cup of coffee Uncle Jack handed me. "You're here early."

Uncle Jack pointed to a chair for me to be seated and join their little group. He looked over at Barney, back at me, and returned to his chair. "Yeah, I guess I don't like rattling around in that big house by myself." He looked off in the distance, peering over the stacks of antiques filling the room.

I looked at Barney and raised my eyebrows. It was relatively recent since Uncle Frank had passed. Those two brothers had been insepa-rable from day one. It must have felt like a part of your body had been removed when your lifelong companion was suddenly gone. I reached over and grabbed Unkie's hand. He looked at me and tilted his head, smiling with pursed lips. "You look so much like her. It's almost as if she is actually here." From as early as I could remember, everyone told me that I was the spitting image of Grandma Luna. At first, I bristled at those comments. Who wanted to be compared to an old woman when you were a young girl? Now I took it as the highest compliment.

"I only hope I can do the bakery justice," I said.

"Tilly, I have a question," Barney interjected. I bet all of Uncle Jack's friends had lots of questions about his niece suddenly showing up on the scene. They were a protective group, and I was sure they were skeptical about a relative coming to take over his business.

"Yes?" I said, drawing out the word into multiple syllables.

"It's really none of my business," Barney started. He stood and grabbed the coffee carafe to refill his cup. He returned to his seat, stirring the coffee with a spoon clinking the sides of the cup. Keeping his focus on the coffee, he continued, "Why don't you stay with Jack? He's got lots of room in that house."

Thankfully, Uncle Jack and I had already discussed this topic. And it was settled, at least for now. I boldly sat up in my chair and said, "I've never really lived by myself. I've wanted to have that experience for a while."

Barney looked at Uncle Jack and shrugged as if silently messaging *I tried.*

I finished my coffee and set my empty cup on the table. "I better get to it. Those cupcakes aren't going to make themselves." I rubbed my hands together. "Uncle Jack, it looks like you've been busy rearranging again." I walked along a couple of tables and noticed several items had been moved. "Maybe my organization system is rubbing off on you." I laughed. That would never happen.

He stood and looked over the many tables displaying everything from 1800's telephones to 1700's typewriters. "No. Why do you say that?"

I turned to see if he was joking. He rubbed his chin. He took several steps between the tables, examining the items. He looked back at me. "Nope, maybe a customer did that." He picked up a couple of items and moved them to a different location. "There," he said and returned to his chair next to Barney, seeming to be satisfied he had righted everything.

"Barney, what's the latest on Cal's death?" Uncle Jack was back to the coffee corner. "That woman we met over there was pretty upset. I think she felt put out because someone had dared die in her building."

"Yeah, I don't think she would take too kindly to you referring to her as *that woman*." Barney chuckled.

My baker workspace was close enough to the coffee corner that I could still participate in the conversation, or at least eavesdrop. I began gathering all of my ingredients and tools in preparation for making the cupcakes. I had two willing taste-testers at my beck and call. Even though they were friendlies, I was still nervous about sharing my work.

"Well, you saw the kite string," Barney continued. "What I've learned is that it's a type that is expensive and that very few people use for kite flying. It's mostly found in competitions. That might narrow down the list of suspects to someone likely to have that."

"Uncle Jack?" I put my hands on my hips and looked around my little mini bakery. I could have sworn some of the supplies I had were previously in different locations.

"Yes, dear?" He stood and peered over a pile of antiques.

"Did you happen to move some of the bakery supplies?" I shook my head. As I looked around the storage, almost everything had been put in another location. I opened drawers and cabinets to locate what I was going to need for the cupcakes. It might take me a half hour just to find everything.

"Well, of course. I wanted to make it easier for you to find what you needed," he said.

Bless his heart for trying. But we would have to discuss some boundaries. He could keep to his antiques and I would keep to my bakery. I braced myself for another scavenger hunt, and I looked for the cupcake pan and paper liners. I knew I had everything, somewhere.

The quiet of the room was suddenly shattered with the sound of an old-fashioned phone ringing. I jumped, spilling my cup of flour down the front of my apron. Well, at least now I officially looked like a baker. I wasn't surprised that Uncle Jack hadn't upgraded his business phone to the twenty-first century. The phone rang a second time, and I lifted my head to see if he was going to answer it.

"Jack, I think that old phone over there is the one that's ringing." Barney stood and gazed at the direction of the sound. The phone rang again. He looked back at Uncle Jack. "Yep. Now I'm sure of it." His eyes widened.

"Oh, it does that every now and then. Ever since I plugged it in about two or three times a week it will randomly go off," Uncle Jack said.

I left my bakery and approached the phone. It rang again. I wiped my hands on my apron and answered it. "Hello?" I looked around at Jack and Barney. "Hello?" I repeated.

Uncle Jack reached my side. "There's never anyone there when it rings. I try to answer when I can." He took the receiver from my hand and hung it up, then picked it up again. "There's no dial tone, so I'm not sure why it rings."

I headed back to continue my baking. "That's kind of creepy."

"That's what the older gentleman said when he brought it in. His wife was tired of it ringing all the time, so he wanted to get rid of it." He picked up the receiver again and held it to his ear for a few seconds, then replaced it on the hook. "I kind of like the character it has. I like to think maybe it's someone from beyond trying to get in touch, and they just keep trying until the right person answers."

Perhaps he was hoping it might be his brother one of these times. My heart ached for his loss. Uncle Frank was in a lot of ways just like Uncle Jack. They both loved life. I missed him too.

"Well, Jack, I need to head back to the office. I'll keep you posted on any developments in Cal's case." Uncle Jack escorted Barney to the door. It gave me the shivers not knowing what happened right next door. I hoped they would soon have answers. I turned my focus to my cupcakes. Having this first batch turn out well would take all of my concentration. And if they did, I planned to take them to Florence as a peace offering. We didn't start off well. And if we were going to be business neighbors, it would be good for everyone if we got along.

CHAPTER SIX

While my cupcakes were cooling, I decided to take a stroll outside. The leader board of the kite competition read the same as before, looking like Burkhart might in fact pull off an upset. With Cal out of the picture they had a replacement judge sitting at the table. Truth be told, I was trying to work off some nervous energy for my first baking attempt in my new space. Even though I hadn't finished culinary school, I had acquired all of the basics. Due to my move from Boston, completing my studies had to be put on hold.

But Uncle Jack made me promise that when I arrived I would let him pay for me to finish school. I agreed but secretly hoped I was so good he wouldn't have to use his money.

My lungs filled with fresh air, I returned to my kitchen to finish the cupcakes. Using the pastry bag full of cream, I loaded each cupcake with the sweet vanilla. This was one area where I planned to experiment with different flavors. I wanted to have a variety to supply customer's requests of cupcakes, frostings, and fillings. The next batch of cupcakes up was almond batter and coconut filling. Why not go tropical since we were at the beach?

I finished filling each one and stood back to admire my handiwork. A few cupcakes had bigger holes than others, but those would just get more frosting to cover the blemishes. And who didn't want more frosting? I topped off each cupcake with the chocolate glaze. I chose the best-looking one, sprinkled a little powdered sugar on for garnish, plated it, and went in search for Uncle Jack. Thankfully, with me in the antiques store now, his absence wasn't as much of a concern that an unattended business would get ripped off.

As Uncle Jack returned from the beach, I met him at the door, sweat beads dotting his bald head. "Whew, it's a warm one today. And I don't just mean the weather. I really think that Burkhart is going to pull off an upset," he said. He looked at my outstretched hands and grinned widely. "Is this what I think it is?"

I matched his smile and nodded. "I want you to have the first one."

He put his hand on his heart. "You should join me. And we should toast this momentous occasion." He led me back to the coffee corner. I wouldn't have been surprised if he had pulled out a bottle of hooch, even at this early hour. I was quickly learning to expect the unexpected from Uncle Jack. He poured us each a cup of coffee. We clinked cups and said "cheers." Uncle Jack inserted about half of the cupcake in his mouth. Immediately his eyes widened, and not in a *this is the best thing I've tasted* expression, but instead in more of a *this thing is hideous* kind of look.

"What's wrong with it?" I asked and scooted to the edge of my chair, looking at the half-eaten cupcake on his plate. At first glance, it looked fine. How could I have messed it up? My face flushed and tears blurred my vision.

He shook his head and held out his hand in a halting gesture, swallowing in a large gulp. He swallowed again as if to rid his mouth of the horrible taste. "No, I think for your first one, it's OK."

It didn't seem OK. And if my biggest fan didn't like it, I wouldn't have any customers. "I don't understand. I followed the recipe to a T," I said. I stood and picked up his plate with the remaining cupcake. I examined it from all sides. It looked moist and delicious. I tossed the cupcake in the trash and the plate with it. I held my head in my hands.

Unkie came up from behind me and put his arm around my shoulders. He quietly said, "I'm sure even professional bakers throw out a lot of their first tries. You'll get it." He wiped a tear from my cheek.

"But if I can't even follow a simple recipe like an amateur, how will I ever be a professional?" I wiped my tears on my sleeve and stomped back to the baking area, slamming things around for the cleanup.

Uncle Jack followed me. "Tilly, give yourself a break, OK?" He stepped around the counter and said, "Here, let me help you."

We silently cleaned the mess. All the while I pouted that I wasn't perfect. So what if I had to keep working at it? Was he right? Maybe if I returned to school and kept at it, I might get better. I had to place all my hopes on that. My dream of Luna's Bakery had to stay alive. Because otherwise... I couldn't let my mind go there. The dishes sat in the dishwasher, and we finished storing the ingredients for next time. I picked up the pastry bag of cream and looked a little closer at it. Normally, with the vanilla flavoring it would be a slight off-white color. But the filling was a bright, stark white. Could that be my mistake? I squeezed a dollop onto my finger and tasted it. Yep, pure shortening. How could I have made that big of a mistake?

"This is it. I held out the bag. Somehow there's shortening in this bag instead of the cream filling I made." I perked up a bit. If I found the cause of the problem, I could fix it. Silly me. I hadn't even tasted one of my own cupcakes. I took a big bite of the chocolate to get some of the filling. My eyes bulged. Gross. I spit the cupcake out and gave Uncle Jack a huge hug. "Maybe I can do this after all." I clapped my hands and took a stuttering breath. OK. That was a good test for how I handled setbacks. An area for improvement, for sure. "Oh, I'm so relieved to figure it out."

Uncle Jack approached me and held both of my hands, locking eyes. "Um, Tilly. I have a confession."

My cheeks sagged. What was all of a sudden so serious? "What is it Uncle Jack?" I took a step closer to him, looking deep into his eyes. My mind could go from zero to catastrophe in about two seconds. I hoped this wasn't some bad news about his health. From everything I had seen, the man was as healthy as a horse. His endurance could certainly outdo me.

"I was only trying to help," he said.

"I don't understand," I replied.

He stepped around me and picked up the pastry bag with the shortening inside, holding it out for me to see. "I thought these bags were for shortening. So I filled them up from the cans to make it easier for you to measure. I guess it got mixed up with the cream filling you made." His voice wavered.

I jumped up and pounced on him with a bear hug, then laughed and held his hand. "Tell you what. Why don't we make a deal? You are totally in charge of the antiques. And I'm totally in charge of the bakery. If the other one would like help, we can offer our services?"

"You're not mad?" he asked.

"I will never be mad at you, ever. Uncle Jack, you have always had the biggest heart for others. From the time I was old enough to come visit you and Uncle Frank, your generosity and kindness were overwhelming."

"I like your suggestion," he said. He grabbed the tray of cupcakes and slid them into the garbage can. "Just like they never existed. I promise I'll stay out of your way from now on."

"If your stomach can handle it, I would still like you to be my taste-tester. But I won't ask you to try anything I haven't first tried myself."

"Deal," he said, and we shook on it.

A loud bang came from the other side of the wall that we shared with Florence's Bookstore. We both looked at each other. "I didn't think anyone would be in there yet. I wonder what's going on?" I asked.

Uncle Jack took off like a rocket. "One way to find out."

I scurried to keep up with him and put some distance between me and that shortening filling. I shuddered, reliving that terrible taste. Never again.

CHAPTER SEVEN

The door to the bookstore was propped open, just like at the antique shop. I was sure it could use some thorough airing out from being vacant. But, you know, from the dead body too. I only hoped we wouldn't find another mysterious situation on our hands. I followed Uncle Jack inside to scout out the source of the noise. He abruptly stopped, and I bumped him from behind, uttering, "Umph."

Furniture filled the entire room, scattered every which way. Bookshelves, tables, chairs. Boxes upon boxes of books. And in the far corner, already completely set up was a fully furnished tearoom. A small round table was adorned with a flowing tablecloth designed with pink roses. Light pink chairs surrounded the table, which had four place settings of saucers, cups, and cloth napkins. Behind the table in the corner was a gold lamp with a beige lampshade and large pink bow.

And towering above it all was an oval mirror that must have been six feet in diameter.

Uncle Jack stepped through the door and panned the room. "Ah, Flo. I mean Florence. There you are." He moved further into the fray, weaving between the piles. "We heard a bang and wanted to see if everything was OK."

Florence wore a different dress from the other day, flowered with pink roses that matched the tablecloth and with two sets of pearls around her neck—and her sensible heels. As sensible as heels could be. Still tucked into her purse was Princess Guinevere. I wondered if she wouldn't mind me calling her cat PG for short. That name was a mouthful. Though I was sure that reference would offend her based on the vibe I got.

She came toward us, stroking her cat. "No. Put that against the wall," she ordered the movers and pointed. She stopped in front of Uncle Jack, her feet planted wide, appearing ready for battle. She looked him up and down. And I would swear she sniffed.

Whether he was aware of the slight, I couldn't tell. But my kind uncle said, "You're making great progress. You'll be open in no time." He looked around. There was a ton of work to do. But judging by the number of people helping, he was probably right.

"No thanks to the neighborhood. That person's body in here almost made me cancel my purchase contract." Princess Guinevere quietly meowed from the bag attached to Florence's shoulder. "But I wouldn't be deterred. This bookstore is my destiny."

Uncle Jack snickered, and his mouth slightly tilted up in a grin. "Are you serving tea?"

Florence turned her head. "Oh, not to you." She halted, possibly realizing how rude her comment was. Or not. "I mean, we will have tea for our book clubs."

I was pretty sure Uncle Jack would have no interest in her book clubs or tea. That just didn't seem like his thing. He said, "We want to wish you the best of luck for your store." He stretched his arm toward her to shake hands.

She looked at his hand and instead returned to petting her cat. "I just hope my Gwinnie recovers from the trauma. She has never seen"—she put her hand up to her mouth, turned away from her cat, and whispered—"a dead body before."

Uncle Jack looked at me, eyes wide, as if to say *this woman's a bit of a loon.* I gave a slight nod.

Gwinnie looked up at Florence, let out a loud yowl, and leapt from the purse. Florence squealed and with both arms reaching tried to capture the escaping cat. The aisles were too small for Florence to make much progress. "She's probably just stressed from all of the drama." Florence looked back at us and touched her hair to straighten the imaginary stray strand. "I need to get back to work. Lots to do," she said and lifted her arm. It appeared her work was ordering the movers around.

She stopped in her tracks, and right in front of her, Gwinnie and another cat were circling each other. Florence looked back at us and pointed at Willie who had invaded her space. Florence's voice raised a couple of octaves she said, "Get your cat out of here! Why do people think they can just come and go in this place?" She took two steps toward the cats, who were now nuzzling each other. "Stop that, you mangy cat. Leave my Gwinnie alone." She reached toward Gwinnie to scoop her up, and the cat stepped just out of reach. "Oh, this is turning into the worst day ever."

The cats moved further back into the stacks of boxes. "Dang, Willie. How did you get in here?" We all turned in unison to the voice coming from the doorway. If the man was referring to Willie, this must be his owner, Justin.

I took a step back and put my hand on my heart. Uncle Jack mentioned the guy renting the apartment above the antique store, but he failed to tell me how good looking he was. Justin had the surfer-guy thing going on. Mussed up, wavy blond hair. Muscles protruding from his snug, short-sleeved faded T-shirt. Shorts and flip-flops. The whole package. The muscles in my diaphragm tightened, restricting my breath. *Simmer down, Tilly.* I took a slow, deep breath and forced my gaze away from Justin.

Florence stormed toward Justin and poked her finger in his direction. "You need to keep your alley cat away from my princess. And out of my store, everyone. We have a lot of work to do." She turned and approached one of the workers, pointing at several pieces of furniture.

Justin moved further into the store, saying, "Geez. She could use some calming beach vibes." He winked at Uncle Jack, as if that was some kind of code. "Hey, Willie." He reached the cats and scooped them both into his arms. "What's this?"

Everyone turned to see what Justin referred to. He held up part of a kite tail that both Willie and Gwinnie had in their mouth, like the spaghetti noodle and the two dogs in *Lady and the Tramp.* The orange ribbon dangled in his hand.

Uncle Jack stepped toward Justin and took the ribbon. Examining all sides, he looked up and said, "That's part of the tail of Maverick's kite."

Florence gasped and her hand flew to her mouth. "Will it ever end?" She whimpered, shaking her head. She grabbed Gwinnie from Justin's arm and stuffed the cat into her bag.

Justin stroked Willie's back. I could hear the purring from where I stood. Willie had a new girlfriend. *Let the games begin.* "The other thing," Justin started, clamping his mouth closed.

Florence's head flew up. "What now?" she yelled.

Justin pointed behind some boxes. In the dust in the corner, it looked like there were some footprints.

Florence pounded her heels in the direction Justin indicated. He touched her arm. "Don't go there."

She glared at him. "This is my store, and I'll go where I want to. Those cleaners obviously did a poor job and they won't get a dime from me."

"Well, maybe that's a good thing," Justin said.

Florence squinted at him.

"What I mean is that one set of the footprints looks like it's a pair of specialty shoes that you wear for gripping sand. Sometimes volleyball players have them. But I've recently seen kite fliers wearing them too so they have some resistance in controlling those large kites." Justin looked around the room as we all stared, like he was giving a performance.

Uncle Jack moved to the center of the group. "I think we all need to get out of here for the time being to let the police return and continue the investigation into Cal's death." He panned the circle, and we were all bobbing our heads.

Florence sniffled and Uncle Jack went to escort her out. "Don't worry. I'll come help you finish moving in after the police give the all clear," he said. That man could sweet talk and encourage the crustiest of personalities. Good thing, since she would be our business neighbor; they would no doubt have a lot of time with each other.

I took a deep breath. Maybe the clues were piling up in favor of one of the kite-flying competitors. It sure looked like an open-and-shut case. I only hoped it would be resolved soon. I didn't have any fear for my safety. But the pallor cast over the town by this mysterious death would not be good for tourism. The workers exited the store, and we followed Uncle Jack and Florence, quietly closing the door behind us.

CHAPTER EIGHT

The sleep of the dead was now a distant memory for me. No amount of exhaustion from the work or sea air to clear my lungs and mind could have provided me any rest last night. I knew adjusting to a new place would take some time. Everything in my little bungalow cottage was new. It was sparsely decorated until I could afford a few more items, but I was insistent that I wanted nothing from my old life. I craved a fresh start. Despite spending money on a quality bed, it had not quite lived up to the advertisement proving better sleep. Perhaps in time.

And the fact that my neighbor kept a few egg-laying chickens in his yard did not help. Thankfully, there was no crowing rooster. But early in the morning I could hear those little ladies taking care of business. Clucking and clawing for food and laying their eggs.

I looked forward to another day of baking, my happy place. The antique shop was only a few blocks from my cottage. I could easily walk the distance but decided it would be the perfect distance to practice a small amount of moped riding. Helmet strapped on and backpack in place, I slowly goosed the accelerator. Before I knew it, I had peeled rubber and was speeding toward the beach. One turn of the handle propelled me almost halfway to the store. I removed my hand from the accelerator to let the machine coast the remainder of the way. My heart raced. Thankfully, no one was harmed in my trial run.

The machine sputtered the last few feet to the front of the store and died. I looked down, hoping to see something obvious causing this, but I knew nothing about motor vehicles. I stepped off the moped and pushed it to a spot out of the way. Great. I broke it already. Or maybe there was some secret button I needed to know about.

"Hey, your inaugural ride. Great job!" Always the encourager, Uncle Jack. He stood in the doorway to the store.

"Except I think I broke it. It died just as I got it here." I removed my helmet and slipped out of my backpack.

Uncle Jack took my helmet and we headed back to the coffee corner. "Let's go see Anna in a bit. Maybe she has some history on that thing that could help. Hopefully, we didn't get you a lemon right off the bat."

I set my backpack on the floor and pulled out a notebook and pen. Unkie handed me some coffee. I inhaled and closed my eyes. "I'm probably going to need several of these to get going today."

"You didn't sleep well?" He sat in the chair on the opposite side of the table.

"Nah, lots going on. And my neighbor's chickens are early birds." I took a gulp of the coffee. Already my brain was waking up.

He reached his arm across the table and tipped his head. "Tilly, give it time. You've had a lot of change in a small amount of time."

I sighed and my shoulders slumped. "I know. But I have big goals. And I'm impatient." I smiled at him.

"All in due time, girl. Don't be so hasty to wish your life away. Enjoy the journey as well," he said. I put my cup on the table and gave him a hug. "And I'm sorry for all of the nonsense next door. That can't be helping your transition."

I sat and took another drink of coffee, finishing the cup. "Well, I'm going to my happy place. Planning the next things I'm going to make. I got to thinking about your suggestion to get my name out there. Later when we come back from the moped shop, let's stop in at Mocha Joe's. I have some ideas to propose." Just thinking about that conversation made my hands sweat. I wiped them on my pants.

"Yes!" he yelled. "I knew you'd eventually come around. I just wish you could see yourself the same as others see you. An extremely capable woman."

"OK. Enough of the mutual admiration society for now." I tapped my pen on my notebook. "I'm thinking I will offer some bran flax muffins." I had found a great healthy recipe that I assumed would be well received. I would source local and organic ingredients as much as possible, which would also allow me to charge higher prices.

"What happened to your sweet treats?" He looked at me, his expression slack, a whiny tone to his voice.

"Uncle Jack, I don't want to send everyone into a sugar high all the time. I'll have those too. But I'd like to offer choices."

"Well, as long as you don't force me to eat those poop producers all the time, I guess I can get on board with that."

I clipped my pen to my notebook and headed to the kitchen. "Deal. But I want you around for a long time." I planned another go at the cream-filled cupcakes, sans my helper filling my pastry bag with shortening this time. Just knowing what happened the first round boosted my confidence. I planned to bake a batch as a peace offering for Florence. I could have Uncle Jack bring them to her to help mend that relationship.

"Can I help you find something?" I heard Uncle Jack say. I raised on my tiptoes to see who had entered the store. I might suggest he add some kind of a doorbell that goes off when someone comes in. Especially if I was alone in the store all the way in the kitchen corner.

"Maybe," the woman said and continued to look along the tables. The intensity of her search appeared as if she was looking for something specific. Uncle Jack followed her from place to place. She stopped and looked at him as if just noticing his presence. She pushed her glasses up and said, "I'm looking for a pocket watch. A very specific pocket watch." She sidestepped Uncle Jack and continued scouring the tables.

Despite the apparent disorganization, Uncle Jack seemed to have a surprisingly good handle on what he had and where it was at. "If you can describe it a bit more, I can tell you if I have it."

The woman turned toward him and pursed her bright red lips. "I don't know how you could have a clue what's in this mess," she said in a condescending tone. She picked up a small birdcage and removed it from the top of a silver goblet.

Uncle Jack stepped forward and took the birdcage from her hand, returning it to its spot. "I'm here to help. Seriously, if you can give me a description, I promise I can tell you if we have it."

She reached into her purse and pulled out a piece of paper, unfolded it, and handed it to Uncle Jack. She pointed to the picture on the paper and said, "I'm looking for the Imperial officer's pocket watch. It's one of the most expensive ever made. Just like that." She tapped the paper for emphasis.

Uncle Jack looked up from the paper and said, "Well, I can tell you we don't have that. But I do have some very nice pocket watches." He turned and started around the other side of the table.

"No," she said. "It has to be that one. And I don't want to buy it."

I was more confused than ever watching this exchange.

Uncle Jack stopped and tilted his head, his bushy eyebrows furrowed.

"What I mean is," the woman started. She followed Uncle Jack and retrieved the piece of paper from him, folded it, and returned it to her purse. She shook her head. "Someone stole this from me, and I'm going around to antique shops to see if anyone sold it."

"I'm so sorry," he gently replied. "If you can give me your name and number, I will be sure to let you know if I see it."

"I'll be back if I don't find it." She turned and left the store.

I left the kitchen and followed the woman's path out the door, looking both ways as I got to the sidewalk. I returned and said, "That was bizarre."

Uncle Jack shrugged. "Maybe. You might be surprised at some of the kooky customers I get in this antique store. Each piece," he said, lifting the birdcage again and twirling it, "has a story." He set it down in the same location the woman had placed it, apparently deciding maybe she had a point with her comment about the clutter.

I wiped my hands on my apron. "Tell you what. After I get this batch of cupcakes out of the oven, let's head to the moped store."

"Mmhmm," he replied, distracted. He picked up a couple things, a typewriter, a stagecoach with accompanying horses and rider, and a brass tea kettle. He arranged them more along the lines of how I would display them, in neat orderly rows. I really hoped he wasn't second-guessing himself because of that woman.

CHAPTER NINE

Thankfully, the delicious aroma of my desserts didn't add to my waistline. I pulled the chocolate cupcakes from the oven and placed them on a cooling rack. I untied my apron and hung it on hook shaped like a little spatula.

"All right, Uncle Jack. I'm ready to head to the moped store." I scanned the room and found him continuing to rearrange like a madman. I had to admit, it did make it easier for people to see what was there. "Looks good," I said.

He harrumphed. I didn't think he wanted to admit that woman had a point, especially given her rudeness. My uncle was kind and forgiving. And I think she hurt his feelings.

I touched his elbow. "This is your business. You get to run it the way you want." I pulled the moped keys out of my backpack. Might as well see if the thing would start, even for just the short trip.

"I don't want anyone ever to say this old dog can't learn a new trick or two." He set the model ship down that he had been holding. He reached over and adjusted its angle. "I've just been reluctant to change much after Frank passed." He further arranged the ship's placement.

"I'm sorry." I put my arm around his shoulders. "I'm sure he would be fine with what you want to do." I looked at him and brushed the escaping tear from his cheek.

"Yeah, he would probably be kicking my butt for waiting so long." He chuckled. "That man didn't mince words." He sniffled. "That's why we made such a good team."

We turned and headed out the door. My initial reluctance at leaving the store unattended waned just the slightest. But I didn't know if I would ever get used to that. I swung my leg over the moped and inserted the key. Uncle Jack looked at me and held up crossed fingers. I turned the key and the engine moaned. I turned it off. It was worth a try.

Uncle Jack took the moped by the handlebars and pushed it as we began our short trek. Even though the kite festival was over, the throngs were just as big. I guess any excuse would get people to the beach. Every time I exited the antique store onto the sidewalk, the soothing sound of the waves hit me. I could easily see how Uncle Jack and Uncle Frank had made this their home for so many decades.

"I'm so glad I moved here," I said and looked at Unkie. He wasn't even breaking a sweat pushing that thing. Though, the mid-eighty degree day was still several hours away and we would be dripping in no time.

"You ain't seen nothin' yet," he replied.

"Should I be worried?" I laughed.

"There's so much here that I want to share with you." He grinned. "That salt-water taffy store." He flicked his head up and to the right. "Daffy Taffy. They have almost a hundred flavors. Just when I've tried them all, they make more."

"You really do have a sweet tooth, Uncle Jack." The taffy store was painted with large pink and white vertical stripes on the side walls. The topmost part of the wall had a horizontal pink stripe with taffy in white wrappers. The door was a light teal, also with taffy in multiple-colored wrappers. They had a large front window where you could watch them pulling the sticky, sweet candy.

"They also have tasting nights when they're trying out a bunch of new flavors. You could do that too. Have a tasting with different kinds of pastry."

I hastened my walk as Uncle Jack was hitting his stride, my breath still catching as I tried to keep up. "I like that idea," I said.

"But," he said and looked at me in all seriousness, "don't do like me and lose your dentures during the tasting. That's not a good look."

I paused, waiting for his punch line. He continued his brisk pace. "OK, so noted," I said and tipped my chin down, hoping he couldn't hear my snickering.

I took a deep breath, trying to generate a second wind before we arrived and I wasn't able to speak at all.

Uncle Jack slowed down and leaned the moped against the railing in front of Nelson's Moped Rental Shop. I followed him inside as we searched for the worker. There wasn't a soul in sight. People here really did have an openness and trust I had never seen before. He put his hand up to the side of his mouth. "Hello, hello, hello," he said in the form of an echo. He looked at me and smiled, finding small joys in every experience.

"Oh, hi there," a male voice said from behind us. "Do you want to rent some mopeds?"

We wheeled around. The nametag on the young man said Cooper. Uncle Jack leaned forward like he was studying the name and raised his head, looking the young man in the eye. "Where's Anna?" He looked around like he expected her to jump out and yell *surprise*.

"Oh," Cooper said quietly, moving behind the counter and fiddling around straightening some papers. "She doesn't work here anymore."

Uncle Jack took a step closer. "Is she OK?" He stretched out his arm, as if to comfort Cooper.

Cooper shrugged. "Yeah. Um, did you want to rent?" He looked at me for clarification.

I stepped forward. "No. We bought a moped the other day, and it's having issues running. I'm hoping you have a mechanic that can take a look at it."

"Sure. I'll have to check Alan's schedule and let you know. Do you have it here with you?"

"Why doesn't Anna work here anymore?" Uncle Jack continued. I wondered where his mind was that he was so concerned about her welfare.

"I really shouldn't be talking about this," Cooper said, fidgeting with his ear. He looked around and leaned in. He mouthed, *she got fired.*

"What? Why?" Uncle Jack demanded answers.

"I'm really going to get in trouble for talking about this." Cooper looked around again. "Can you show me where the moped is and give me the keys?" His look implored me to stop the grilling from Uncle Jack. He took the keys and I led us to the sidewalk.

"I'll take full responsibility," Uncle Jack said.

Cooper inhaled and huffed. His jaw muscles flexed. He must have concluded that the only way out of this was through it. Once last covert glance around and he blurted, "She was badmouthing the owner and his business. I guess she just did it one too many times."

"Does it run at all?" Cooper asked me.

"It sounds like it will start but then doesn't," I said. Explaining car things was way outside my knowledge and expertise.

"Let me talk to the manager or Nelson. I know I can get her job back," Uncle Jack pleaded.

Cooper had both handlebars of the moped and began pushing it around the corner to the back of the building.

"Nelson is just the business name. It's actually owned by Cal Borman." Cooper let go of one of the handlebars and gripped his left hand around his neck. He turned and disappeared with the ailing moped.

"That poor girl," Uncle Jack said. He plopped onto the bench with his head in his hands. "She needed that job. I have to see if there's something I can do to help."

"I know you mean well. But I don't know if getting a disgruntled employee rehired is the best choice. Maybe it was a blessing in disguise for her to move on to another place."

He shook his head, running his fingers through his thinning hair. I put my hand on his back and lightly patted.

"Maybe. I'll think about it." His body slumped. Dejected, he said, "We should probably get back." And we were off.

CHAPTER TEN

Without a word, we proceeded on our return route to Checkered Past Antiques. I figured we would stop by the coffee shop another day. That gave me relief and would mean I could do some more experimenting before making a business deal.

On a dime, Uncle Jack pivoted ninety degrees to the left and entered Mocha Joe's Coffee Shop. I stood outside, stunned. I put my hands on my hips and waited. When he realized I hadn't followed him inside, he came back to the door.

The neon outline of a steaming cup of coffee blinked in the front window.

"No time like the present," he said, grinning. He bounced on his feet, waiting for me to budge. My stomach was in my throat. Maybe it was the best time. No chance to get any more nervous than I already was and try to back out at the last second. I gulped and stepped inside. There wasn't a smell much better than fresh ground coffee beans and fresh brewed coffee. I followed Uncle Jack to the counter.

A man about forty years old was behind the counter serving a customer. He wore a light blue button-down shirt with sleeves rolled up to his elbows. Over the top was a bright orange apron that said *Mocha Joe's Coffee Shop*.

Uncle Jack and I waited our turn, and when the man saw us, he burst into a giant smile. "Hi Jack," he said and then turned to me and said, "You must be Tilly."

I nodded, unable to utter a word to this gorgeous guy. Uncle Jack looked at me and put a hand on my shoulder. "Tilly has a business proposition to talk to you about." He continued to look at me.

After an awkward amount of silence, I cleared my throat, "Um, yeah. I have a business proposition for you, Mocha Joe."

He chuckled. "You can just call me Joe. I'm excited to hear it. When Jack mentioned you were moving to town and opening a bakery, my wheels started churning. I think you've got a lot of potential for multiple avenues of business around town." He removed his apron and came around the counter. He grabbed a notebook and pen and pointed to a table along the wall. "Why don't we sit for a minute to chat. Callie can take over for me for now." The teenage girl looked at us and grinned to show a mouth full of braces.

We followed Joe to the table and sat. I tried to inconspicuously inhale deeply to calm my nerves. I couldn't tell if they were frayed due to the business discussion or the fact it was being held with a good-looking man. I was in no way interested in dating for quite some time, if ever.

Joe sat across from me and Uncle Jack sat to my side. "I just want to say, I hope you don't judge our quaint little town by the recent events," Joe said. "Any updates, Jack?"

Uncle Jack shook his head. "Not much. There's been a few clues found. It's pointing to someone involved in kite flying from what I can see. But Barney is keeping the good stuff close to his vest for now."

"I'm sure we'll know soon. On to happier stuff." Joe smiled at me. "Why don't you go first, Tilly? I'd love to have your input before I bombard you with my hairbrained schemes."

"Joe, you're too modest. You've got excellent business sense, from what I can tell," Uncle Jack interjected. He looked at me. My turn. *OK brain, please click in so I don't look like a total fool.*

I scooted my chair forward and put my hands in my lap. "I haven't gotten everything worked out yet." Joe sat forward with his elbows on the table, the notebook and pen pushed aside. "But I've got a few ideas. I'd like to offer options for pastries that are locally sourced and organic, along with the classic items. But I'm very open to what you think would sell." There. I didn't totally flub it, I hoped.

"Great," Joe said. "That's just about what I was thinking."

"I knew you two would be a great match," Uncle Jack said. Joe and I swiveled our heads toward him. "In business, I meant." He held up a hand.

My face was now on fire. I needed to quickly exit. "How about I bake up some samples and bring them by? You can choose a few you like to start with and we can go from there." Somehow I was able to carry on a sane conversation.

Joe stood and held out his hand. "I should get back to work," he said.

I shook his hand, holding it just slightly longer than socially acceptable for a platonic shake. *Oh boy.* "Thank you for your time. I'll be in touch." I touched Uncle Jack's arm and guided him outside. The fresh air hit my face for a reality check. I quickly took off toward the antique shop.

"Whoa there," Uncle Jack said, jogging to catch up to me. "I have to say, you're already getting in better shape."

I kept silent and tried to retain my brisk pace. If I did so, I might just keel over by the time we got back. I slowed down a notch. "I think that went well." I was grateful he pushed me outside my comfort zone, but I didn't want to say that to encourage him further.

"I agree. I think he likes you," Uncle Jack said.

I stopped, mostly for emphasis but also to catch my breath. "Uncle Jack. Do not go fixing me up. It will be a long time before I want to pursue a romantic interest."

He held up his hands. "OK. Message received. It might not be on my timeline, but Cupid has his own." He snickered and took off.

Oh boy. Well, I said my piece. We continued silently on our walk, Uncle Jack considerately slowing to match my pace.

"You just never know when the love bug will hit," he said. His tone implied he had something up his sleeve.

I didn't want to get into a disagreement with the man who had so lovingly taken me in during the worst time of my life. His heart was huge and always in the right place. Perhaps with fewer years left on the earth, he was becoming more of a romantic. I let his comment go by. He was quite insightful, but I more than had my hands full with the bakery.

As we neared the antique shop, he stopped and pointed to the end of the harbor. "Do you see the lighthouse?"

I looked in the direction he indicated. "Of course."

"The top level has been converted to a small, charming restaurant. Just perfect for two lovebirds," he said and sped off for the final distance to the shop.

"Uncle Jack!" I admonished and shook my head, following him.

Inside the store, he busied himself in the corner opposite the bakery.

I said to him, "Don't think I don't know what you're doing." We both smiled, and I bounced over to the kitchen to fill my cooled cupcakes with cream. This time, I would taste it to be sure it was the right stuff. Lesson learned. My mind wandered to Joe. I just couldn't let myself go there yet. But could I be disciplined to remain focused on my business? Time would tell. I smiled as I finished preparing the cupcakes. If I could spend every day like this, I would be in heaven.

CHAPTER ELEVEN

I stopped and looked in the small mirror that hung next to the door in my cottage. I pinched my cheeks, wanting to make sure this was all real. My life was nothing like it was just a few short months prior. I had my own adorable place to do just as I wanted. My eye for design had so far garnered me a bed, a small table and chair to eat at, a love seat, and a television. The TV had only been on a bit each morning as I got ready for work. I couldn't bring myself yet to just be in the quiet. My brain needed some background noise.

The stress lines around my eyes had noticeably diminished since I had moved to Belle Harbor. I chalked it up to the sea air. But spending time with one of my favorite people on the planet contributed significantly to my disposition. Today, I had to walk to the shop since the moped was still being repaired. I cherished the time to gather my thoughts along the way. They had settled down after Joe and I had made several pages of notes last night. My plan for our collaboration was coming together. If this was successful, I had even more ideas percolating about other business deals.

At this hour, the beach was sparsely dotted with the early risers. Experiencing life in a vacation venue had to put a positive spin on things. If it didn't, why would you live here?

The door to the store was open, and Uncle Jack and Justin were deep in conversation. "And speak of the devil." Uncle Jack lifted his head when he saw me enter. I ignored his comment.

"Hi guys." I waved. "You're here early, Justin." I slipped off my backpack and stood next to them.

"Yeah, I'm looking for that little rascal again. For the life of me, I can't figure out how he continues to escape," Justin said. He started weaving through the aisles, looking under tables. "I just hope he's not causing any trouble."

"He's welcome anytime after what he did finding those clues to Cal's death. Barney wouldn't say, but I got the feeling that may have broken the case wide open." Uncle Jack was a bit dramatic. I didn't see how a piece of a kite or some footprints in the dust could lead to anything. But a kite flier who was used to always winning? Would that be enough to make someone angry to kill the judge? I shuddered. It sounded like Cal may not be well liked with employees bad-mouthing him and his business. It did explain a bit about why my moped pooped out. I only hoped Uncle Jack hadn't wasted his money on a lemon.

"We can keep looking for him if you need to get to work," I offered.

Justin looked at Uncle Jack and back at me. He came around the table and stood next to us. "Nah, Justin makes his own hours," Uncle Jack said and winked at Justin. "That's how it is in the agriculture business."

Justin giggled. "Sure, Jack. But Tilly's right. I should be going. I'll stop in later to see if you've found my little guy." He headed to the door and almost collided with a customer rushing in.

The man's clothes were disheveled, and I suspected that he may be a homeless person. His wool plaid shirt was overdressed for the weather. His construction style pants were worn and dirty. He turned to see Justin leave and came further into the store. I pulled out my phone in case I needed to dial 9-1-1. Big city life had taught me well in situational awareness. The man reached into his pants pocket and pulled out something he gripped in his hand with a chain dangling. He looked at the open door again, and back at Uncle Jack.

"What do you have there?" Uncle Jack inquired.

The man looked at me, then around the room. "A watch. Do you buy these types of things?" he asked. He held his arm out, cupping the timepiece.

I took several steps toward the duo, my phone remaining at the ready.

"May I?" Uncle Jack asked.

The man looked at him and nodded. He carefully transferred the watch to my uncle. I could see an intricate design along with writing on the cover of the watch. Uncle Jack clicked it open and some type of red jewels sparkled from inside the watch. He gently closed it and handed it back to the man. He rubbed his chin. Pointing to the watch, he said, "That's a bit above my pay grade, but I have a lot of dealers that I can contact to see if they're interested."

The man jammed the watch back into his pants pocket. "I don't need to see a dealer. What could you give me for it?"

"Well." Uncle Jack crossed his arms. "The problem is if I buy it, I don't really have a clientele that could afford it."

The man took two steps toward the door. My instincts said Uncle Jack was slow-dancing this guy somewhere. "OK. When can you get in touch with the dealer? I'm kind of in a hurry."

"Give me a day or two. Just a sec." Uncle Jack turned and headed to the cash register.

The man's eyes darted around, scanning the other items on the tables.

Uncle Jack returned with pencil and paper. He handed it to the guy and said, "Write down your name and number, and I'll let you know when I have something for you."

The guy looked down and shook his head. "I'll come back. I need it soon, though. My mother is sick and she needs the money for her treatment." He turned and almost ran from the store.

"Uncle Jack," I said.

"Don't worry, Tilly. I've been doing this long enough. That's the exact watch the woman was looking for the other day." I followed him back to the cash register. "There's obviously something fishy between the both of them."

He picked up the phone, dialed, and grinned. I think he was maintaining calm more for my sake. My heart raced just as if the guy had come to rob us with a gun. This was not the life I had envisioned in a happy, little beachside town.

"Yeah. Barney. Jack. Got a lead on that watch. Guy just came in with it. I put him off, but I'm sure it won't be for long. He wants to dump it ASAP." Uncle Jack nodded. "All right. See you soon." He hung up the phone and rubbed his hands together. "We're going to nail that jerk. Nothing much peeves me more than people stealing. Well, that and murder." He gestured to the wall we shared with the bookstore. "I got a feeling Barney is going to make an arrest soon."

It wouldn't be soon enough for me. The not knowing was hard. From my perspective, the crime against Cal was personal. That gave me the smallest amount of solace that I wasn't in danger. But if someone killed once, would they do it again? And this sketchy watch gave me concern for Uncle Jack. If he did this guy wrong, no telling what people desperate for money would do.

CHAPTER TWELVE

I headed back to the kitchen and my happy place. Cupcakes never stole or murdered. The worst thing they did was add to my weight, and I'd take that risk all day long over fear for my life. I got the bowl of cream from the refrigerator and spooned it into a pastry bag. I squeezed a dollop onto my finger and tasted it, just in case. I closed my eyes and swallowed it. Mmm. Sweetness. I lined up the cupcakes on the counter and started at the left end, poking a hole in each cupcake and squeezing it full of filling. I continued on until I had the two dozen cupcakes filled and ready for the icing. I had made a batch of chocolate ganache to top them off. Never too much chocolate in my book.

"Hey there," I heard Uncle Jack call out as Barney arrived. Our little town police chief seemed to be a regular at the antique shop. Never mind that he and Uncle Jack were old friends and poker buddies. This had to be the most excitement in Belle Harbor in quite some time. "Thanks for coming so quickly. You know, my memory for details ain't what it used to be." He chuckled.

"What are you thinking, Jack? Is the watch hot?" Barney asked. "Hi Tilly." He waved to me in the kitchen.

I waved back. "I'll have fresh cupcakes to sample in a bit."

"Barney, I don't know if you're more interested in the stolen watch or getting dibs on the cupcakes," Uncle Jack said. "I think Tilly's bakery is going to be good for my antique business too." He looked at me and smiled.

"That is, if we don't eat all of her profits." Barney chuckled.

Uncle Jack pulled out a piece of paper and handed it to Barney. He pointed at it. "Here's the watch the guy brought in. I found this online. Likely worth about twenty Gs."

Barney whistled and looked up. "I might be in the wrong business."

"Has anyone reported it missing? A woman was in here a few days ago looking for that same watch," Uncle Jack said.

Barney headed back to the kitchen, followed by Uncle Jack. They watched me frost the cupcakes. "Nope," Barney said. "I think I'd remember that. But there's a lot going on. That investigation into Cal's death is keeping me and my deputy pretty busy."

"What's the latest?" I asked.

He continued his observation of my work. "Well, for starters, we've interviewed the other judges in the kite competition. And with Cal's shady business dealings, there's a lot of people that appear to have a beef with him. It's more complicated than I expected."

I handed him a cupcake. There wasn't going to be any further progress on the investigation until he got one of these in his belly. He put almost half of it in his mouth, leaving a cream-covered mustache.

"Oh, for heaven's sake, Barney." Uncle Jack handed him a napkin. I handed my uncle a cupcake, and he followed suit, taking a huge bite.

I gave him a napkin. "I'm going to have to put a quota on you two."

Barney rolled his eyes. "These are just too good. One more? Then I promise I'm done. For now."

"OK." I slid one across the counter with another napkin. "But I need some left over to take next door."

Barney snapped his head up. "You mean to Flo?"

"Don't let her hear you refer to her that way. She made it clear that it's Florence," I said. I finished icing the last cupcakes and began loading a dozen of them into a box for delivery.

"Of course," Barney said, wiping his salt-and-pepper mustache again for good measure. "Do you know what her situation is?" He looked back and forth between Uncle Jack and me.

"Barney, you old devil," Uncle Jack said. "Don't tell me you're smitten with her?" He reached for another cupcake, and I tapped his hand and shook my finger at him.

"Smitten? What are you? Out of the 1920s?" Barney replied. "I'm just asking. I didn't see a ring on her finger."

"Well, maybe you haven't lost your investigative skills after all," Uncle Jack said. "That's very observant of you."

Barney headed back to the front of the store and started mindlessly picking through items on the tables, picking up an antique schooner and holding it up high. "Maybe I'll buy this. I have just the perfect spot for it," he said.

"Don't try to dodge the subject, my friend." Uncle Jack followed him. "Spill it," he said.

"She seems nice enough. And I like to read. So I think we would have something in common," Barney said, avoiding all eye contact, continuing to look the ship over from all angles. He moved to the cash register, set it on the counter, and got out his wallet. I didn't know if he really wanted that, but he was willing to spend money to get the subject changed.

"Barney. You old dog. Good for you," Uncle Jack said. He played along with Barney, took his money, and packaged up the ship to go.

"I hope that looks just like you want it to in your house." Uncle Jack smirked.

Barney took a couple of steps in my direction. "Tilly, why don't we go out to celebrate you opening your business?"

"Oh, you don't have to do that. I haven't done much yet. Except make Uncle Jack sick with the first batch of cupcakes," I said.

Barney looked at Uncle Jack and back at me and grimaced.

"Don't worry. There was a mix-up in the cream filling. But as you tasted, that's all been corrected," I assured him.

He nodded. "Well, I think that's a success." He looked at Uncle Jack. "Why don't we take her to Fiona's? She could stand to meet someone her own age since she's just been hanging out with us two old codgers," Barney said.

"Hey, speak for yourself," Uncle Jack countered. I was convinced he didn't think of himself as old. And he certainly didn't act his age. "But yes, Fiona's would be great. And I think they would get along well."

"Now that you two have my social calendar filled, why don't we pay Florence a visit and deliver these cupcakes?" I asked.

I held out the box for Barney to take. He looked at Uncle Jack and said, "Not a word." He took the box, and we followed him out the door. For the life of me I couldn't see Florence as much more than an eccentric cat lady. But beauty was in the eye of the beholder. I tried to imagine Barney and Florence as an item, but my brain wouldn't go there. I hoped for Barney's sake that she didn't break his heart. He was a gem, too, and one of Uncle Jack's best friends. The two of them had been inseparable since Uncle Frank had passed. And I was grateful to Barney for that. Maybe I would whip up a batch of cupcakes just for him. We hadn't started off on the right foot with Florence, and I hoped the cupcakes would be a sufficient peace offering. And if she had any interest in Barney, his delivery of them would just sweeten the pot.

CHAPTER THIRTEEN

The appearance and ambiance of the bookstore had been transformed from the cluttered mess of moving day. Walls held shelves lined with nicely arranged books, nothing out of place. In between the shelves were overstuffed chairs with ottomans and side tables holding rustic lamps. Each little nook looked like a cozy reading corner where you could cuddle up and spend hours with a good book.

The center of the room was dotted with small round tables holding books on display. The tea corner in the back of the room still looked ready to host the first gathering.

Barney led the welcoming committee boldly into the store. Florence had her head in a box and looked up as we approached. Barney held the box of cupcakes in outstretched arms to show that we came in peace.

She looked from Barney to Uncle Jack and me and back to Barney. She raised up and asked, "Can I help you?"

Barney forged ahead. "We brought you a welcome to the neighborhood gift. Actually, Tilly made them." He flicked his head in my direction. "You get to taste the most delectable treat you've ever had."

Florence accepted the box and set it on the counter. That woman still had her game face on. I didn't know what it would take to get her to crack a smile. "Thank you."

"Maybe you could serve them with the tea," Barney suggested as he looked at the tea set up in the corner.

"No, we'll have the traditional biscuits with our tea." Florence returned to unpacking the box in front of her.

I felt like we were being dismissed. I turned to leave, making eye contact with Uncle Jack. He nodded his agreement at the sentiment.

"I love *The Great Gatsby*," Barney exclaimed.

Florence swung her head up from the box. "You do?" She stepped from behind the counter and picked up the book that was displayed on a stand at a nearby table. She thumbed through it, looking at Barney as if to assess his sincerity.

Barney took a step back, his face flushed. He rubbed his hands together. "Sure do. I enjoy many of the classics."

Florence joined us in the center of the room. Gwinnie sidled up to her, rubbing her leg and purring. Florence scooped her up in her free hand. "Maybe you would be interested in joining a book club. We'll have a new one every month," she said softly.

"Yes, I would," Barney said. He took a step closer to Florence. "Look, I'm really sorry for how things started here. We've almost finished our investigation into Cal's murder."

I looked at Uncle Jack, who shrugged. As far as we were aware, there was progress with clues and suspects, but Barney made it sound like an arrest was imminent. My money was on the disgruntled kite flier. When ego and money combined, many times it led to no good. But in this case, the end result was dire.

Florence looked down and returned the book to the display. She stroked Gwinnie, whose purr was now the loudest sound in the room. Florence looked up at Barney, her demeanor returning to a more serious tone.

Barney continued, "You don't have anything to worry about. It wasn't a random crime. I'm certain you're safe here." He reached to pet Gwinnie, who resoundingly hissed at him.

"Oh, Gwinnie. Be nice to the man," Florence said. "She's just shy. I'm sure in due time she'll come around." The tips of Florence's mouth hinted at a smile. *Well, I'll be.* Barney was our secret weapon to crack the hard shell of Florence. Who knew? Florence's disposition returned to a serious tone. "I just can't get the sight of him out of my mind. I mean, the way he was laying there. Not moving." Her hand covered her mouth.

Barney approached Florence and stood on the opposite side from where she held Gwinnie, his hand on her back. "That must have been horrible for you."

Florence nodded. She put her hand over Gwinnie's eyes, as if reliving the scene. "And for Gwinnie."

Barney attempted another pet of Gwinnie, tentatively reaching his hand behind the cat's back. He gave two small strokes as a trial run. "She really saved the day. Without her and Willie finding the pieces of the kite in here, we might not be as far down the road on the investigation as we are."

Barney was laying it on thick. But Florence was eating it up. I was going to be curious how this relationship developed—if it did. All signs right now pointed to a little spark being ignited. Maybe that would spur Uncle Jack on to finding a love. I worried about his loneliness. I would be on the lookout for a suitable companion. Two could play at this matchmaking game.

"Well," Uncle Jack interjected. If either of us didn't interrupt, we might never get out of here. "We should probably get back to the antique shop. Barney? You coming?" Uncle Jack moved to the door and I followed him.

"I'd love to know how you like the cupcakes," I said to Florence.

Florence and Barney pivoted as if our presence had alarmed them. It was all I could do not to chuckle. Barney was likely in store for a lot of razzing from Uncle Jack.

I looked around Barney and said to Florence, "I would love the opportunity to provide the tea biscuits for your events." I held my breath, bracing for a bristled response. All she could say was no. And I was trying Uncle Jack's advice of taking action and putting myself out there before I was ready. I closed my eyes for a second.

"Hmmm" was Florence's response.

Well, that wasn't what I expected. I didn't know what to do with that response. "Please think about it and let me know. I'm happy to bring you a sample if you'd like," I offered.

"Thank you for the welcome cupcakes," Florence said to Barney. He opened his mouth, closed it, and smiled. "And come back again to get signed up for the book club. We're going to start soon. I'm really looking forward to bringing some culture to this place." Florence swept her arm in a half-circle, implying the town could use highbrow activities. She followed the three of us out the door. From the sidewalk, I peered through the window of the bookstore to see

Florence smiling big. She turned and swayed back to the box she had been unpacking when we arrived. We might just end up being friendly business neighbors after all.

CHAPTER FOURTEEN

I t was more of a brisk morning than I expected on my walk to the moped store. My ride had been repaired and was ready to be picked up. The coolness of the air did wonders to clear my head. With my latest batch of cupcakes, my confidence was increasing in my baking skills. I was proud of myself, so boldly offering to provide the tea biscuits to Florence. No doubt she would be a tough customer. But it would make me work that much harder to ensure they were top quality.

I rounded the corner of the moped building to the wide-open beach. Seeing the expanse of the ocean always gave me perspective. My time here in Belle Harbor, while quite exciting in many ways I couldn't have predicted, was just what I needed at this point in my life. And I couldn't be happier to be here with Uncle Jack. I opened the door to the moped store, and Cooper lifted his head up from the paperwork on the counter.

I raised my arm and waved. "Hi Cooper. I'm here to pick up my moped."

He scanned the room, as if looking for someone or something. I followed his glance to see what he was looking at. Nobody else except me was inside the store. I stepped to the counter and pulled out my wallet. "How much do I owe you?"

He shook his head and held out his hand, again looking around. What was I missing? I couldn't figure out what he saw. "You don't owe anything," he said.

"Of course I do. You fixed the moped. That must cost something." I opened my wallet and got out my credit card.

"No. The amount of lemons Cal sold was staggering. Now that he's gone, we are trying to do right by the customers."

"Wow. OK." I slipped my credit card back into its slot. "That's very nice of you."

"It's the least we could do. And can you tell Jack that it looks like Anna might get her job back?" He reached behind the counter, pulled out a set of keys, and handed them to me. "She was only guilty of telling the truth. And thankfully, that helped to put a stop to those horrible business practices." He escorted me to the front of the store to the lineup of mopeds on the sidewalk.

"He'll be so happy to hear that." I took the helmet from Cooper, stepped onto the moped, and inserted the key. I looked at Cooper and turned the ignition. It fired right up. He gave me a thumbs-up and I rode away.

I had only ridden this thing a couple of times, but already I felt like I was getting the hang of it. Thankfully, it was just a short jaunt to the antique shop. Not many people were out yet. I decided last second to stop at Mocha Joe's, say hi, and pick up some coffee for Uncle Jack and myself. I slowly decelerated and pulled the moped to a gentle stop in front of the coffee shop. Uncle Jack's foresight to buy a moped with a basket on the back for deliveries was genius.

Mocha Joe and two other employees were behind the counter serving customers. I waited my turn, and when I arrived at the counter, Mocha Joe said, "Tilly! What a treat to see you. I'm ready for those pastries when you are. Let's do it." His exuberance gave me energy. I smiled at him, not sure if it was the caffeine or his natural positivity.

I laughed. "You got it. I'll be in touch soon. For now, just a couple of drip coffees to go."

Joe quickly grabbed two travel cups and pumped them full, placing lids over the steaming liquid.

I paid for them and asked, "Would you please also put them in a travel carrier?"

"Of course," he said and handed everything to me. "Tell Jack hello." He waved and moved over to help the next customer.

I carefully placed the coffee on the back of the moped and strapped the carrier into the basket. Crossing my fingers, I turned the key and it started right up again. Two for two. This was shaping up to be a great day. I sat tall on the seat and motored my way toward the antique store, visions of muffins in my head. I had just the recipe in mind that I wanted to try next for Mocha Joe's. Suddenly I realized I had come upon a person to my left that I didn't see until the last second. I swerved to miss her. The coffee from my basket flew, covering her entire right side.

She screamed, "Look what you've done. You idiot! Watch where you're going."

I stopped the moped and pushed it up against the building. "I'm so sorry. Here, let's go into my uncle's store. I've got some towels I can use to dry you off."

She looked up, and I recognized the woman from the other day who had come to Checkered Past Antiques looking for her stolen watch. The same watch that guy had come to sell a few days afterward. She brushed off her clothes, trying to remove the brown liquid. She scowled at me with daggers in her eyes. I hoped I hadn't just cost Uncle Jack a customer. And my day had started off so well.

She followed me into the store. I stopped when I got in the door, not expecting the scene I witnessed. Uncle Jack was there with Barney and the guy from the other day with the expensive pocket watch in handcuffs.

"What?" was all I could get out. I looked at Uncle Jack for an explanation.

He looked at me and then at the woman behind me, dripping with coffee. He tilted his head and furrowed his bushy brows.

"I had a little accident. I'm going to get some towels to help her clean up." I turned and looked at the woman again. "I'm so sorry." I headed back to the kitchen.

Uncle Jack stepped to the door, blocking the entrance. "You're just in time," he said.

I turned around, confused by his statement. "In time for what?" I asked, then realized he wasn't talking to me.

Barney stepped forward and began with the Miranda rights, "You are under arrest for the murder of Cal Borman. You have the right..." He turned the woman around and cuffed her.

She tipped her head down. "This isn't fair. If that loser hadn't sold me a lemon, it wouldn't have broken down. And my precious watch that was supposed to fund my retirement wouldn't have been stolen by that lowlife when I had to go for help." She sobbed into her chest.

My eyes bulged as I looked at Uncle Jack for answers. Was this the conclusion to Cal's murder? Were we safe now? Why would someone commit murder for a stolen watch?

The door opened again, and Barney's deputy arrived. He nodded one time toward Barney, silently acknowledging the plan. The deputy held the woman by her left elbow, and Barney took the man as they escorted them from the shop.

I moved toward Uncle Jack. "I don't understand."

He chuckled. "Barney put two and two together about the watch and traced it back to the woman. As soon as the guy came back to sell the watch, he had me call the woman to come get it. I had no idea his plan was two birds with one stone."

I put my hand on Uncle Jack's arm. That was a lot of drama for one morning. "Are you OK?"

"Are you kidding? We just nabbed a thief and a killer. I'm on top of the world. Now"—he started toward the back of the store—"we just need to get your business off the ground."

I stood where I was. "How can you be so calm about that?" My heart continued to race. I was pretty sure with my adrenaline level I could outrun anyone at this point.

"Ah, pish. Just another day at the office." Uncle Jack started arranging a table of antiques. It was starting to look a little more orderly after all.

I didn't understand how he could be so nonchalant about it. But I tried to follow his lead. Next up on my list for baking was the healthy muffin recipe. I only hoped I wasn't in for cardboard flavor with this flax and bran combo. Getting back to some baking would calm my nerves.

CHAPTER FIFTEEN

The music thumped in the background as the hostess led us to a booth. Fiona's was a bar that, from the looks of it, was a popular watering hole. Barney, Uncle Jack, and I took our seats as the hostess placed waters, drink coasters, and menus on table. The back wall illuminated a large display of liquor bottles. Three televisions hung above the display, showing various sporting events. Customers filled the horseshoe-shaped bar. A younger woman wearing a baseball cap serving drinks waved at our table. Barney and Uncle Jack returned the gesture.

"This place has great energy," I said, picking up a menu. And many good bar food choices. A lot of comfort food. Just what I needed.

"Wait 'til you meet Fiona," Uncle Jack said, smirking. I wondered what I was in store for this time. He seemed to want me to experience more adventure. Truthfully, I was ready for a little dullness after everything that had happened since I arrived in Belle Harbor.

"What's good here?" I asked, running my finger along the choices on the menu.

Barney looked at me. "You can't go wrong with a burger."

"No, you can't. Hi guys. And you must be Tilly." The woman reached across the table to shake my hand. "I've been looking forward to meeting you," she said. "And what took you guys so long to get in here?" She play-punched Barney in the arm.

"Fiona, we've been a little busy," Uncle Jack said.

"I've heard! Why don't I get you started with a round on the house of our specialty paloma cocktail?" She looked at each of us as we nodded. Fiona left to fill our order.

"I can see why the place has energy. She's great," I said, taking a sip of water.

"I'm glad you think so. I thought you two might hit it off. And you can finally have someone your own age to hang out with instead of us old geezers." Uncle Jack tipped his head back and laughed. It was good to see him relax for a bit.

"Hey!" Barney said. "Speak for yourself." Those two had such great banter.

"Yeah, I guess. You did mastermind the takedown of those two the other day," Uncle Jack said. "Spill the beans, how did you know who killed Cal?"

Barney took a long swig of his water, for what seemed like a dramatic pause. "Well, first, everything made it look like Maverick had done it. Motive was a bit weak, but sometimes it's the smallest thing that's the final straw that sends someone over the edge."

Fiona brought our drinks and placed them in front of us. The pinkish-colored drink in a highball glass bubbled. "Here you go," she said. "Stacy will be here in a jiffy to get your orders. Enjoy."

I took a sip of the refreshing cocktail. It was a nice, smooth combination of tart and sweet. The woman knew her stuff.

Barney continued, "It just didn't sit right with me. I've known that kid since he was little. He's got a temper, and no doubt he's competitive, but I couldn't envision him as a killer."

I held my drink glass close to me, nursing it to the bottom.

"I can see that, now that you say it. But how in the world did you ever trace things back to the woman?" Uncle Jack asked. I looked over at his glass, and the drink was gone. If we didn't pace ourselves, Fiona would have to wheel us out of here.

"I took a step back and looked at Cal's life. It didn't take me long to see that his businesses were a huge source of conflict for many. His customers and employees."

"Ah, yes. Anna. I'm glad you're the one who has to connect the dots. I couldn't do your job." Uncle Jack held his arm up, signaling Fiona for another round.

"I do love me a good puzzle. Once I started digging into his recent business transactions and looking at each customer, a pattern began to emerge. I'm actually surprised something hadn't happened to him sooner as despicable as he was. Not that getting scammed in a business deal is any reason to murder someone."

Uncle Jack nodded. "Life's too short to get that upset about things."

Stacy arrived with our second round of drinks and took our order, burgers all around.

"I put my usual chart together on the board with the victim and suspects. When I noted a motive for each one, the strongest driver came from the woman he sold a lemon to. It wasn't her first car from Cal."

"But a lot of people bought lemons, like me and Tilly. We didn't take it out on Cal by killing him," Uncle Jack said.

I tipped my glass up and finished my first round. I was beginning to feel the effects of the liquor and relaxed a bit.

"Right. But once you follow the money, a couple of people popped up to the top of the list. And the final piece is when you called about a guy trying to fence that stolen watch."

Uncle Jack shook his head. "You're hurting my brain with all of that." He laughed.

Fiona arrived with our burgers piled high next to a mound of fries. My eyes were bigger than my stomach. But I was going to attempt finishing the entire thing.

"Hey, Tilly. We've got a tasting night coming up at the bar. Why don't you come?" Fiona asked.

"That's what I'm talking about," Uncle Jack said. "A girl's night out."

I looked at Fiona and said, "I'd love to. Thank you."

"Great!" She squealed and clapped her hands. "You two are welcome to come too." She pointed to Uncle Jack and Barney.

They both shook their heads in unison and said, "No way."

"Ah, we're not that wild," Fiona said. "Maybe I should host a senior night just for you two."

Uncle Jack and Barney looked at each other wide-eyed. "Really?"

Fiona laughed. "Well, I was joking. But maybe it's not that crazy of an idea after all." She looked over her shoulder at the growing crowd. "Gotta go. Tilly, I'll be in touch. You two"—she pointed at Barney and Uncle Jack—"stay out of trouble."

"Well, that's not gonna happen," Uncle Jack said. I had no doubt he meant it. My life in Belle Harbor was not what I expected. But it was just what I needed.

~ele~

Read on for a mysterious letter from the past, gut punching muffins, and funky smelling clues in ***Muffins and Misdeeds***

MUFFINS AND MISDEEDS

A Belle Harbor Cozy Mystery

Book 2

CHAPTER ONE

I switched off the TV and plunked into the lone chair in the cottage. The sparsely furnished room cried out for more pieces to appear like someone lived here. The wide-open windows beckoned the ocean air and sound to permeate the place. I wanted the full ambiance of beach living to envelope every aspect of my life. My move to Belle Harbor from Boston was intended to begin anew. And it was off to a great start.

Upon my exit from Boston, I left everything behind that I could. Certainly my ex and his new girlfriend. How was I to know that when I decided to enroll in culinary school that he would hook up with the instructor? I always wondered if that was payback in some way for my bold move to follow my dreams. He was never one to be supportive of much of anything other than what he wanted. Our life together had begun as a fairytale. He was from a prominent family, attended good schools, and was the perfect choice for my mate. I was so swept up in the fantasy I lost myself in the mix.

If not for Grandma Luna's urging from her deathbed to follow my heart, I would not be in Belle Harbor. She was always one to set the trend. And it was usually not what everyone else was doing. Her free spirit was the guide for her life.

My parents were not fans of Grandma Luna. Their references to her hippie ways and lazy lifestyle always hurt my heart to hear. She was an amazing baker who owned a thriving bakery. Her friends and neighbors adored her, and she was generous to a fault, giving back on a regular basis to the local homeless kids. It was no doubt her hippie-looking appearance set my parents off. She changed her hair color monthly and dressed in outlandish clothes. She was by all accounts a very colorful character, not concerned about what others thought of her life. I secretly admired her moxie and wished for just a dollop of that to land on me.

I was sure my mom's choices in life were deliberately in direct opposition to everything my grandma would have done. My prim and proper mom attended an Ivy League school to become an attorney. In the process she met my dad, who hailed from a prominent family. If she had a checklist of criteria for her ideal life, she would have ticked off every single item, right on schedule.

Circumstances deviated her from that roadmap as soon as her children arrived on the scene. Despite the overbearing parenting, neither my brother nor I fit into our parents' mold. It wasn't for lack of their trying to develop a mini-me. We attended private school, wore uniforms, and signed up for extracurricular activities to rub elbows with the elite.

At some point around middle school, my mom concluded that all hope was lost for her kids. She had been shipping me off every summer to visit with Uncle Jack and Uncle Frank in Belle Harbor. Just like my grandma, those two were living their best lives. The pull I felt toward that life ran deep. But it wasn't until the culinary instructor incident that I finally chose for myself.

I was now on a path to open my own bakery just as Grandma Luna had done many years before. Surprisingly, I felt an emptiness for parts of my former life. I did miss my parents. And my loving younger brother. But establishing my own identity and life was now my priority.

Uncle Jack had welcomed me with open arms. His Checkered Past Antiques shop sat along the boardwalk on the beach. He and Uncle Frank had run that store for as long as I could remember. With Uncle

Frank's recent passing, I was glad that the timing of my move could provide Uncle Jack some family company. He graciously renovated a corner of his shop for my temporary baking kitchen.

Today, my new friend Fiona was meeting me at Unkie's shop to look for items to decorate my cottage. I was all in for the beach theme and would take just about anything. Except for the small mirror by the door, my walls were bare. My teal-colored chair patiently waited for more furniture to fill the room. Truth be told, Uncle Jack had antiques toppling over one another. He couldn't say no to an estate sale, always a sucker for more history. I think he liked the stories behind the pieces as much as he did selling them.

Uncle Jack and his friend Barney, the chief of police, had taken me out for a celebration to Fiona's bar. Those two were in the matchmaking business, and in this case I was all in. Fiona was my age and full of energy. I had a feeling we were going to be great friends.

I looked around the room to size up what might be needed to make it feel more like my home. The white shiplap walls needed color. And if I wanted to entertain at all I needed more seating. I wouldn't find that at the antique shop, but Uncle Jack had plenty of decor in his inventory to get me started.

The sounds of the sea soothed my mind. They were a far cry from the horns and sirens of the big city. And my neighbor's little barnyard of chickens had become a gentle, lulling background noise. Last night at my arrival home on my moped, I had to dodge a couple of those wandering hens.

My phone buzzed. I stood and pulled it out of my pocket. Fiona was already at the antique shop, setting aside some things for me to look at. I hoped she had a better eye for design than I did. Left to my own devices I might not get much further than what I already had. Simple and minimal spoke to me.

I grabbed my backpack and latched the window so it remained open just a crack. My confidence had eked up a notch with my baking skills. And I was really looking forward to delivering the muffin samples today to Mocha Joe's. I needed to get a cute name for them because calling them bran flax muffins wasn't going to make them fly off the shelves.

Partnering with Joe was my first business collaboration. I was nervous about the reception of my product, but what was the worst that could happen? Nobody would like them and I could try something else. My ego would take a hit, but I was determined to be persistent toward my goals.

Thoughts of Joe made my stomach gurgle, and not just from the anxiety about my baking. I shook my head free of those thoughts. I couldn't go there, not with so much on my plate with building a new life. I swung my leg over the moped seat, started the engine, and headed the short distance to Checkered Past Antiques.

CHAPTER TWO

I powered down the moped and leaned it again the front wall of Unkie's antique shop. Thankfully, after that first malfunction it had been running like a charm, and I was getting the hang of maneuvering it. A low murmur of voices drifted through the open door. I peered through the window and saw Fiona and Uncle Jack with their heads together over one of the antique display tables. I grabbed my backpack and headed inside.

"Hey, you two," I said on my way to the back of the store.

Uncle Jack took a step back, placed his hand over his heart, and steadied himself. "Whoa, Tilly. Give an old guy a heart attack."

I deposited my backpack and helmet and joined them. They had placed a small card table in the middle of the aisle along with a couple of items for me to look at. "Sorry about that. You guys have been busy."

I picked up a large rusty anchor with a small rope through the hole at the top. It was large enough to go on the wall or stand on my mantle above the fireplace. "This is cool," I said and put it back down.

Fiona looked up, her face slack, far from her normal vim and vigor. I looked at Uncle Jack. His face mirrored Fiona's expression.

"What's wrong?" I asked and placed my hand on Fiona's arm.

Neither said a word. Uncle Jack picked up a round piece of sea glass and situated it next to the anchor on the small table. He shook his head.

"I'm just bummed," Fiona started. She stepped away from the table. "I heard this morning that Kevin Packton was found dead in his pig pen."

I turned my head toward Uncle Jack for an explanation. He seemed to know everyone in town. "Kevin owned a local distillery. Sandbar Distillery is a little ways out of town. They've been in existence for a long time."

"I'm so sorry," I said. "Do they know how he died?"

Fiona shook her head. "I mean, he was a rival of our family's distillery. But there's no way I'd ever want him dead. Their business did really well and was just about to go international."

"And..." Uncle Jack started. He picked up a second piece of sparkling blue-green sea glass and set it next to the first.

The ocean-colored orbs started to roll off the table. I grabbed them both to avoid another tragedy. They would look adorable displayed on a white tray on a coffee or side table.

"Spit it out, Unkie," I ordered.

He took a deep breath. I wondered if they had been friends. As he aged, my uncle had lost a few in his friend group. That must've made you wonder sometimes if your number was coming next. "Barney hinted that based on the evidence he was murdered."

I shivered and goosebumps sprung up on my arms. Our town police chief Barney was besties with Uncle Jack. They were like brothers. I was grateful that Barney hung around so much after my Uncle Frank had passed away. Unkie jokingly complained about it, but I think he secretly appreciated the comfort of his friend.

"I can't say too much," Uncle Jack said. I didn't want to push it. The details would come out soon enough. And we had a task to do. "Let's get back to decorating that cottage of yours."

"You don't have to do this, Jack," Fiona said. She held up a lighthouse lamp. "This is cute." She set it next to the anchor. "And Tilly, you can nix any and all of our choices. You have to live there, so this should be your decision."

I scanned the stacks of antiques for something I could use to hold the sea glass. "I like what you have so far," I said. I seized a large bowl and put it on the table with the sea glass inside. "I like the glass. Let's see if we can find some other shapes to go with these."

The three of us silently picked through the hodge-podge of items. "What all are you thinking you want?" Fiona asked.

"Not sure," I said. "I like the variety we have so far. Let's just keep looking." I held up a small china cup. "Unkie, what in the world is this?" The cup had a shelf inside covering half the cup and a hole in the shelf. I turned it around to get a good look at it.

Uncle Jack chuckled. "That's a mustache cup," he said and starting rummaging through another stack of items on a table against the wall. "Here it is." He held up the matching pair.

I swiveled my head toward Fiona. Her eyes widened and she shrugged.

"A what?" I asked.

Unkie joined us and held out the cup. He pointed to the inside and said, "These started in the 1800s. That part inside was designed to keep the mustache away from the hot beverage."

"Well, I guess that makes sense." I shrugged and handed him the cup.

"Men used to wax their mustaches to keep every hair in place. And when they drank hot liquids, the wax would melt into the cup. These keep that from happening." His face was dead serious. I waited for the punchline.

I turned toward Fiona so Unkie wouldn't see me cracking up. "I guess I don't need those. But now you at least have a pair you can sell."

Uncle Jack ambled over to a shelf near the front of the store. Window shoppers could see the displayed wares. He arranged the two cups next to a stack of small plates with a similar pattern.

"Do you think you have a whole set of dishware in here with that pattern?" I asked. Uncle Jack's organization system was nonexistent. He hypothesized that customers looking for antiques like to hunt for treasures. And that discovery was just as much an enjoyable part of the journey as the actual find. Maybe. But ever since our new business neighbor who owned the bookstore had described the place as junkie, Uncle Jack had been slowly getting more orderly. I think the comments stung, but subtly he made a few small changes almost every day.

I stepped next to Fiona to continue our search. I didn't disagree that it was intriguing to explore the wide variety of items on the tables and shelves. I could see how people would spend hours here.

"Oh, this is fun," Fiona said. "I think my grandma might still have one of these." She carefully hoisted an ancient typewriter out of the stacks. "I don't know if it will go in your cottage. Maybe I'll get it for myself." She held it up, rotating it in her hands. She set it on the card table and pressed several of the letter keys. "Seems to be in good shape." She hit the carriage return and a small piece of paper jutted out from the top portion of the carriage. Fiona bent to get a closer look. "I think it's an old letter." She gently tugged to release the paper.

Uncle Jack joined us and looked over Fiona's shoulder. The faded letters were difficult to make out. "May I?" Uncle Jack asked and held out his hand. He pulled the paper within inches of his nose. "It says something about if you find this, you need to investigate the property on old Highway 99 next to the old cattle farm."

"What does that mean?" I asked. Two mysteries in one day.

"I don't know. But I think that's near the Sandbar Distillery." Uncle Jack looked at Fiona. "May I keep this? I think we need to call Barney. It may be nothing but doesn't hurt to get it checked out."

"Of course," she said. "Do you need the typewriter too?" She picked it up and held it out.

He shook his head. "Maybe just to be safe. I'm going to get on the horn with Barney," he said and walked away.

"Why don't we call it good for now?" I said. "I think this is a good start. And I need to get started on the muffin samples I'm making for Mocha Joe's."

Fiona's chin was on her chest, obviously distracted by the suspicious death of Kevin.

I reached out my hand. "One step at a time. I'm sure Barney will figure it out."

"I know. It's just hard to take. Kevin and I had discussed some exciting collaborations...." Her voice trailed off. She looked at me. "Let's talk happier stuff. I'm having a tequila tasting at the bar tomorrow night. Say you'll come," she said, reaching out her hand.

I smiled. This was going to be a beautiful friendship. "Fiona, I wouldn't miss it."

CHAPTER THREE

"What's on the docket for today, darlin?" Uncle Jack asked. I had arrived early at the antique shop to begin baking the muffins I planned to take to Mocha Joe's today. I loved my little corner kitchen that Uncle Jack had created for me in the back section of his shop. For now, it was just right. But soon I planned to increase my production, and I would need a much bigger space.

I hoped today was a happier start than yesterday after learning about Fiona's friend being killed.

"I'm making the Morning Muffins," I said. I had the second batch in the oven.

"Is that what smells so good?" He stepped over to the cooling rack and pointed.

I loaded the dishes into the dishwasher and put the ingredients away. "Yep. Why don't you try one? They're great with coffee."

He tipped his head up toward me. "Are you trying to trick me with something healthy?"

I snatched a muffin and extended my hand. "You have to sample it before you can say you don't like it. Besides, it's not going to sound good if word gets out that my uncle won't eat my muffins."

He looked down. "Is that carrots?"

"Eat it!" I laughed. "Look, I'll have one with you. I'll even go first."

He took the muffin and examined it by all angles. "I guess if I get the good stuff, it means I have to try these too." He headed to the table and chairs and poured himself a cup of coffee.

I joined him and began peeling the paper from my muffin. I took a bite and saw him slowly studying the muffin. You would think I was asking him to eat dirt. He sipped his coffee and nibbled. He took another drink and a nibble. His gaze lifted to meet mine. I knew he would probably like it, but the suspense was killing me.

"Mmmm," he said and smiled with crumbs in his beard. He ate the remainder of the muffin in two bites. "You got me. Those are deceptively good."

My body tingled, my confidence growing. I might be able to make something of this business after all and do Grandma Luna proud.

"Just don't tell people they have bran and flax in there," Uncle Jack said in all seriousness.

"OK." I pursed my lips to keep from laughing. "I'm going to package these up and head off to Joe's. I'm optimistic they will do well."

I moved to the kitchen and started boxing up the muffins. Uncle Jack followed. I held out another muffin for seconds. He quickly grabbed it and peeled the paper. I turned away so he couldn't see my wide grin. No comment.

"After Mocha Joe's, what's next?" he mumbled with his mouth full.

I closed the box. "One step at a time," I said. Putting myself out there didn't come easily to me. Especially since I was such a new baker. I really couldn't judge my success by Uncle Jack's and Barney's reactions. The real test would come with paying customers who didn't know me.

Uncle Jack took a napkin and wiped his mouth, peering down to see what crumbs had fallen into his beard. "If I know you, Til, you've already got big plans."

I fidgeted with the pile of napkins and the empty muffin tin liners. I shrugged. "I do have some ideas. But I just don't know."

He waited, staring me down.

I continued to straighten the already straight baking tools on the counter. "I would like expand into catering. But that's a whole other deal on a larger scale," I said.

"I knew it!" He turned and headed for another cup of coffee. I followed. "I'm here for you. Just let me know what you need for that expansion."

We both turned our heads to the sound of something falling in the opposite corner of the store. We hadn't heard anyone enter, but in some areas, the stacks of antiques were high enough to hide a small person. We looked at each other and Uncle Jack held out his arm to halt me in my place. He wove through the aisle on the opposite side of the sound.

Moving toward the noise, he said, "Just as I suspected." He scooped up Willie and righted the tipped-over vase teetering on the edge of the shelf. "I think this little guy spends more time here than he does upstairs."

I realized my heart was racing. I inhaled deeply to calm my nerves. "Maybe you should just give him a bed here and make it official," I said.

"Not a bad idea," Uncle Jack replied and sat with Willie on his lap. "Better to make him at home so he doesn't venture next door to

Florence's Bookstore." Willie lifted his head and closed his eyes as if he was imagining the comfy new digs.

"Yeah, she wasn't too keen on Willie fraternizing with her fussy cat," I said. I grabbed Willie and placed him on my lap. His purr rumbled throughout his body.

"I can smell those delicious cupcakes all the way down the sidewalk." Barney made his way to join us in the back of the store.

"Don't let that fool you. She's trying to get me eating healthier with some—" Uncle Jack hesitated.

I glared at him. *Don't you dare call them poop producers.*

"Muffins," he finished. Message received.

"Right on time. I'll get you a sample," I said. I put Willie on the floor and headed back to the kitchen.

"What brings you here so early?" Uncle Jack asked.

I handed the muffin on a napkin to Barney, who inhaled it in two bites. "Another winner," he mumbled. He finished chewing and swallowing and dabbed his mouth with the napkin. "I thought we could rummage through and see if there might be any more clues besides that letter you found."

Uncle Jack shrugged. "Sure. I'm trying to remember what else might have come in from that estate sale at the same time as the typewriter." He wandered around a few aisles until he stopped and started

117

moving some items. Barney joined him and watched the process. "I think it was from the Jefferson sale. But it was quite a while ago." He retrieved the card table from the back of the store and began placing items on it to make room. "It was an eclectic collection. Really just a few things but quite the variety." He grabbed an ornate wall sconce and held it up to the light. "This beautiful Tiffany fleur-de-lis might have been from there." He put it on the small table and continued picking through the mountain of merchandise.

This wasn't just a store with products to sell. These were memories and stories of people's lives. I joined the duo as they dug further looking for more clues. I picked up the sconce from the small table. I felt the pull from my former life. Our home was filled with this style of decor. My chest tightened. That life seemed so far away now. My ex-husband insisted that we decorate in a high-society lifestyle. My own home appeared more like a museum than a residence. The fussiness of it made it hard to be comfortable.

I put the piece down and shook off the memories. "I'm going to leave you two for the scavenging and head out to Mocha Joe's."

Uncle Jack must have observed me with the sconce because he said, "Be patient, dear."

I smiled.

"Here's the early bird crew." Justin bounded into the store. Uncle Jack's upstairs neighbor rented the apartment above the antique store and was Willie's owner. Well, as much as anyone can *own* a cat. "Just checking on my little guy. I think you're going to have to charge him rent soon if he keeps invading your space."

Uncle Jack tipped his head back and laughed. "As a matter of fact, I am going to set him up a little place in the corner. Make it official. He's more than welcome."

Willie meandered into the conversation, and Justin picked him up. "That's kind of you. Just let me know if he gets to be any trouble. Hey Tilly." Justin waved to me in the kitchen corner. "Well, I'll leave you all to your business. See ya 'round." He turned and headed toward the door, then abruptly stopped and pivoted. "Oh, yeah. See you tonight at the tequila tasting, Tilly."

I almost dropped the box of muffins, which wouldn't have been my first disaster since arriving in Belle Harbor.

"Um, yeah," I muttered. I was looking forward to a no-stress evening with Fiona. Now the stakes were raised with the hunky, surfer dude also in attendance. My shaking hands grabbed the muffin box, and I secured my grip. I followed Justin from the store, my mind completely distracted. The salt air hit my face and startled me back to the present. I put my game face on for my business meeting with Joe. Let's hope he liked the muffins.

CHAPTER FOUR

I slowed my pace to gather my wits about me. Mocha Joe's Coffee Shop was a few doors down the sidewalk from Checkered Past Antiques, and I wanted to be composed for my first official business transaction. The waves gently washed onto the shore, the sound soothing my nerves. The neon sign in the window of Mocha Joe's blinked a welcome to customers. I peeked through the glass to see Joe and his employees serving coffee like a well-oiled machine.

I pushed the door open with my backside and entered the store. Customer chatter obscured all other sounds. I had never seen Joe's coffee shop empty. I hoped that was a good sign for my baked goods as well. I found a two-person table along the wall and sat down with my box of muffins. Joe raised a hand with one finger in the air, signaling he would join me in just a minute.

I wiped my moist, jittery hands on my pants. I sat tall to allow maximum air into my lungs. I closed my eyes and visualized my muffins soaring off the shelf while the sound of families gearing up for a day at the beach warmed my heart.

"Sorry about that," Joe said.

I jumped, a little embarrassed I got caught with my eyes closed. I sat on my hands for a few seconds to still my racing heart. "No worries." I looked around. "Are you never not this busy?"

Joe followed my gaze and smiled. "I love it. I figure I'm just adding to the happiness of the community. So what do you have?" He looked at my box.

I opened the lid. The warm, comforting smell of the muffins escaped right on cue.

"Mmmm. They look great! Do I see carrots in there?" Joe looked up.

"Yes. They are on the healthier side, but don't let that fool you. They are incredibly moist and flavorful." I took a muffin from the box and situated it on a napkin in front of Joe.

He took a bite and his eyes widened. *Oh no. What could possibly have gone wrong? I double-checked everything!*

"Are they OK?" I asked.

"Tilly, they're excellent," he said and finished the remainder of the muffin. "They're going to fly off the shelf. What else can you supply?"

"Really?" I asked. I wasn't quite prepared for more. Or, let's be honest, I wasn't prepared at all. "Ummmm." I paused. "I do have my grandmother's cream-filled cupcake recipe. They're pretty good." I sat on my hands again, steeling my nerves. This was progressing much sooner than I had expected.

"Let's start with both the muffins and cupcakes. How about two dozen each, Tuesdays and Thursdays? Can you do that?" he asked.

"Yes!" I practically yelled. Was this really happening? Was my bakery actually going to make money?

"What's your price?" he asked. Of course he wanted to know what they cost—a normal business question that I was completely unprepared for.

"Well, honestly, I hadn't gotten that far." I nervously chuckled. My brain needed to kick into gear before I looked like a complete amateur. "How about fifteen dollars a dozen?" I bit my tongue, scared of the response. Was that way out of line? Would I even make a profit at that price point? I had such a steep learning curve for both my baking and my business. *Note to self: pick Uncle Jack's brain about running a business.*

"Perfect," he said and scanned the room full of customers. He glanced back at the counter and must have decided his employees had things well under control.

"If you have another minute, I have a question." I was sticking my nose in other people's business. But I wanted to help out my new friend Fiona. She was so down about Kevin's death. I swallowed. My face warmed. I forged ahead. Looking around the room, I asked, "You're always so busy here. I was wondering if you happened to hear anything about the"... I lowered my voice... "murder of Kevin Packton." I was convinced my heart was going to pound right through my chest.

He shook his head and crumpled the napkin in front of him. "That's so sad. And scary too."

"Did you know him?" I asked.

Joe sighed. I hoped I wasn't causing him distress with the questions. "Yeah, it's a small town. And an even smaller number of business owners." He scooted his chair back. I assumed our conversation was done and did the same. He continued, "I have a fondness for his family and that business. When I was young, we lived next to the Jefferson Distillery. It was no longer in operation at that point. So us kids would go play hide-and-seek behind the old stills and barrels in the field."

I didn't move. If he kept talking, he might just share something that could clue me in to the mysterious death. "I'm sorry," I said.

"This is a pretty tight-knit community. When something like that happens, it feels like a part of your family is gone." He pulled the box of muffins to his side of the table.

"Even in my short time in Belle Harbor, I'm beginning to quickly understand that. Uncle Jack found a letter in an old typewriter at his shop that had some cryptic note about clues at the old distillery. Do you know what those might be?"

He rose from his seat and grabbed the muffin box. I felt so close to a break in the clues. Would he be forthcoming?

I stood, waiting until the last second to say goodbye.

"There's a lot of rumors about what happened at the Jefferson place during prohibition. I don't know what might be folklore or what might be the truth. It's all probably somewhere in between." He bowed his head, then looked at me. "It wasn't long after Jefferson was shut down that the Packton Distillery started."

The door opened to another large group of customers looking for their caffeinated beverages. Joe held the box up. "Thank you for these. And I can't wait for the cupcakes. Gotta get back to work." He scurried to the counter to care for the crowd.

"Thank you for the business," I said. Did he know more than he said? If this town was so small that when one neighbor sneezed, another said bless you, then someone knew something.

I scooted along the perimeter of the room to get to the door. When I hit the sidewalk, I exhaled a long breath. This bakery was happening. Uncle Jack would be so proud of me. I slowly strolled back to the antique shop, pondering my newfound information from Joe about the distillery. I wondered what that letter meant. Maybe it was a joke? Or in fact a clue to a decades-old family mystery.

I stopped at the railing along the sidewalk, leaned up against a post, and crossed my arms. The waves were in a gentle mood this morning, slowly lapping the shore. The beach filled with families and vacationers escaping from reality. Belle Harbor was becoming my escape from my former life. My new friend Fiona had invited me out, and Justin was also going to the tequila tasting. I smiled. Was Justin just another friend? Was there something else there? Too soon to tell. And too soon for any of that.

My priority was my business. And of course, my uncle. I turned and headed back to give him the good news. I had my very first order. I knew for sure I could make the muffins and cupcakes. I daydreamed about more. I had so many ideas, and I couldn't wait to try them all.

CHAPTER FIVE

The heels of my short boots clicked on the sidewalk as I approached Fiona's. My floral, jersey-knit swing dress brushed my knees, and my navy cardigan sweater hung over my arm. I had gone home after my day to change clothes before coming to the tequila tasting. My work clothes smelled of delicious baked goods. But I still wanted to get out of them and change my mindset for a fun evening. Truthfully, my feet were accustomed to wearing Converse and were revolting against the more formal boot wear.

When I had seen the caramel-colored boots in the shoe store window I had no idea where I had planned to wear them. I only knew that they were adorable and something I never would have chosen in the past. That meant I had to have them. I deserved to enjoy what I wanted in my life. Tonight would be another celebration at Fiona's.

After the excitement from my first sale to Mocha Joe's, I had spent the day planning. I needed to get on a regular schedule for grocery shopping and baking. And I looked forward to experimenting with crumpet baking. I was determined to soften the bookstore owner up with my samples for her tea and book club.

The door to Fiona's was wide open, inviting the ocean air in and letting the joyful sounds of good times out. I stepped inside and scanned the room. The booths were filled with customers enjoying their meals. The horseshoe bar in the center of the room held one empty seat. Fiona called and waved me over. I draped my sweater over the back of the chair and sat. I had only ever been to wine tasting back in Boston. My ex insisted the high-brow bottles were the only alcohol allowed in the house.

"Tilly, I saved the seat for you," Fiona welcomed me. "And you look great!"

My face warmed. I wasn't one for attention. "I'm so glad you invited me." Justin was located to my right. He sat up straight and turned toward me with a comforting smile. How could I be so nervous around him but so relaxed at the same time?

"I think you're going to enjoy this," he said.

I looked at Fiona. She shrugged as if she hadn't arranged for me to sit right next to Justin.

Fiona clapped her hands. Her eyes darted toward Justin and back at me. She and I would have a conversation later. A new friend? Great. A new love? Not so much right now.

"Do you know Anna?" Justin gestured to the younger woman sitting to my left.

I hadn't even noticed her when I sat down. She stuck out her right hand to shake. "Nice to meet you," she said.

"Anna, this is Jack's niece who moved from Boston. She's opened up a bakery," Justin said.

"Well…" I held up my hand. "I haven't—"

"I adore that man. I'm so glad you're here now that Frank has passed," she said.

"Alright, everyone," Fiona began. "Tonight in our tequila flights we have a blanco." She pointed to the clear liquid in a tulip-shaped glass. "Next, we have an extra-anejo." She held up the glass containing an amber liquid. "This is my favorite. It's aged more than three years, proving that good things take time."

"That's my favorite too," Justin leaned over and whispered to me.

"Finally, the mezcal, made from the agave plant." Fiona set the glass back on the wooden display holding all three tequilas. She set it in front of me and smiled. The bartenders filled glasses for the remainder of the tasters seated at the bar.

I sat back in my chair, my brain finally kicking in. "Wait. Are you Anna that used to work at the moped rental store?" I asked, turning to my left. I mean, how many Annas could there be in this small town?

She nodded, her long blonde ponytail, held in place by a loose tie, bobbed up and down. "I was. Until that jerk Cal fired me." Her hand flew to her mouth. Her eyes widened.

"Yeah, I hear he didn't make many friends," I said.

"Well, good riddance to that place. They said I would get my job back, but I never did. I'm meant for bigger and better things, anyway," she said, flipping her head back toward her drinks.

I reached for my first glass of tequila. The middle amber-colored one spoke to me. I picked it up and held the glass out to clink with Justin and Anna. "Cheers." I sipped a small amount. The flavor warmed my mouth like my childhood favorite cinnamon Red Hots candy. My eyes watered, and I set the glass down.

"That one is unique because you can only age it in barrels with no more than six hundred liters," Anna said.

I looked at her and then Justin. That was quite the random fact to know. Justin laughed. "Anna knows her stuff about tequila."

She shook her head. "You'd think it would be enough to get hired on at a distillery. But noooo," she said, drawing out the word. She placed her arm on the bar and rested her chin on her hand, leaning toward

Justin. "And that's so nice of you to say, Justin." She batted her eyes in the most obvious flirtatious manner.

"How's it going, you two?" Fiona had made her way to our side of the horseshoe. She looked back and forth between Justin and me, grinning from ear to ear.

"I've only tried the middle one. But I like it," I said. "Thank you again for inviting me. This is a nice break."

"My favorite is the mezcal," Anna blurted loudly, holding her glass as high as her arm would stretch.

Fiona adjusted her baseball cap, refusing to acknowledge Anna's outburst.

"Justin, what do you think of this one?" Anna held her arm in front of me, as if Justin couldn't see what she referred to.

"I think I'm with Tilly. Extra-anejo it is for me too," he said in a quiet voice.

"You two are adorable." Fiona looked back and forth between Justin and me.

Anna returned the glass to the wooden display with a thud. The liquid sloshed out, discoloring the light oak. She stood, looked around, and huffed. Quickly she took her seat, bumping me in the process. Her light green hair tie escaped and her long blonde hair flowed over her shoulder. I couldn't tell if that was a move to get Justin's attention or an accident. She picked up the tie and placed it on the bar, leaning into my space and staring at Justin. She was getting no traction but didn't appear to take no for an answer.

"Tilly," Justin started. He looked down, then back at me. I gulped. His tone implied a question that I wasn't sure I was ready for. "What do you say I show you the town? You can get to know some of the local activities."

I studied his face, unsure if I was being asked out on a date. It would be fun to have some more adventure. Though, Uncle Jack did provide quite a bit of that. He kept encouraging me to spend time with people more my age. Why not?

"Sure. That sounds nice," I said, still not clear whether this was a date.

"One of my favorite things to do is get out on the water," he said. That was evidenced by his muscled, surfer physique.

I shook my head.

"Well, we can do something else if you want," he said.

I realized he thought I had declined his request as I attempted to remove the distracting thoughts from my brain. "No. That sounds nice."

Justin grabbed one of his glasses, sipping the remainder of the tequila. "Great. There's a kayak rental that we can use to head out into the bay," he said.

I heard another glass thump onto the wooden tray to my left. From my peripheral vision, I could see Anna's three glasses from her flight were empty.

"Hey everyone," Fiona was calling the tasters to attention. "Thank you again for coming. Our next event will be game night." Fiona distributed small plates around the bar with fresh fruit, guacamole with tortilla chips, and cocktail meatballs.

"Yes!" Anna yelled. "I can't wait for that. I cleaned up last time."

What a wonderful evening. Just what I needed. Next time I planned to arrive early enough to get a seat away from Anna. She obviously had designs on Justin, and I didn't need to be caught in a middle-school drama.

CHAPTER SIX

I spent the day in my happy place. My first batch of muffins and cupcakes were delivered to Joe's. Would I ever not feel like an impostor? I had so far to go before I felt like I had an official business and I was a professional baker. Dropping out of culinary school didn't help the situation. Though, getting that degree didn't guarantee I would be a success. The true test would be what Joe's customers thought of the pastries. There was no better feedback than those eating the goods.

I had promised Uncle Jack when I moved here from Boston that I would return to culinary school. Grandma Luna had paid my tuition and I at least owed her that much. I only hoped when I delivered my second batch to Joe that he had good news to share about how everyone raved about my work. OK, at this point, I would take them not getting sick. Or even not complaining. Raving fans would come in time.

Fiona had arranged for her manager to cover the bar tonight so we could have some girl time and work on decorating my cottage. After my baking, I had scoured the local furniture stores to find another chair and side table. Eventually, I wanted to have more than two seats to accommodate a larger group. My friend circle was growing, and I looked forward to having a get together at some point when I was more settled. The treasures from Uncle Jack's antique shop were stashed in the corner until Fiona and I could decide how best to display them. I might be all right at baking, but I had nowhere near a decorator's eye. I didn't know if Fiona did either, but at least we could brainstorm ideas together.

While I waited for Fiona to arrive with our takeout, I grabbed a notebook to continue my bakery planning. I enjoyed this part of the process almost as much as whipping up the next batch of treats. Cupcakes, check. Muffins, check. Cookies? That was next up. I planned to surprise Uncle Jack at his poker party with his good ole boys. That would be a good way to trial. I was pretty sure they would eat anything, though. Cakes. Hmmm. The cake business was somewhat of an entirely different animal. Cakes offered an opportunity for a lot of creativity, but they were also a pretty big commitment. Maybe I would add those when I was busy enough to hire an assistant.

A loud knock rattled the front door, startling me from my quiet planning time. Through the window I saw two large takeout bags in Fiona's arms from Tuscany Grove. I was enjoying time with my new friend. Her energy was contagious. And she was nice to boot.

I opened the door and reached for one of the bags. "Hey. I'm so glad you're here," I said and led the way into the kitchen. "Italian sounds great. What did you get?"

Fiona pulled the boxes from the bag and garlic filled the entire room. "I got us a couple of salads and spinach ravioli with pesto."

I went to the cabinet and got a couple of plates. We started dishing up the servings. "Thank you again for your help decorating. I really have no idea what I'm doing."

She laughed. "Happy to do it."

We moved to the living room and dove into our meal. "I really do need to get out more and explore the town. Are all of the restaurants this good?" I took a bite of the ravioli and savored the flavors.

Fiona tucked her legs under her on the chair and leaned on the arm. "Tuscany is excellent. They have a fried ravioli that I'm thinking of adding to the bar menu."

I choked on my mouthful and my eyes watered. I swallowed and said, "You had me at fried." My muscles relaxed as I thought about how my new life was shaping up in a beautiful way.

Fiona smiled big. She was so easy to be around. The clucking from the neighbor's chickens coupled with the gentle ocean waves provided soothing background ambiance.

"I'm so sorry about Kevin. I haven't heard a word yet from Barney regarding any theories. What do you think happened?" I treaded lightly, not wanting to upset Fiona.

She kept her head tipped over her plate, moving the food around with her fork. "Honestly, I'd rather not think about it right now." She lifted her head. "What I really want to know..." Her voice trailed off.

I chuckled, knowing full well what she hinted at. I cut a small piece of the ravioli and put it in my mouth. I saw from my peripheral vision she continued to stare at me. I slowly chewed and swallowed, not sure what to say. I wasn't even sure what I felt. "For one thing, it's not a date," I said, still averting my gaze from Fiona. "He's just taking me on a kayak ride as my new friend." I peeked at her.

She untucked her legs and readjusted in the chair. "OK. You might not see it yet. I won't push."

"Even if I was interested, I might have to fight Anna for him. Did you see the way she fawned over him at the tasting?" I asked.

"She's not his type. She's too pushy. Hopefully she moves on soon. It really annoys me how she behaves trying to get his attention." Fiona moved to the kitchen to rinse her plate. "If you aren't having any more, I'll box this up and put it in the fridge."

I joined her in the kitchen. "You'd assume I would have dessert on hand at all times. I wasn't thinking. Sorry about that." I rinsed my plate and put them both in the dishwasher, then got two high-ball glasses from the cupboard. "I do have ingredients for the paloma cocktail, if you'd like one of those."

Fiona laughed and returned to the living room. "Well, yes I would. Thank you."

I gathered the tequila, lime juice, Squirt soda, and my written recipe. I had Googled it after my first visit to Fiona's where she had served their signature cocktail. The taste was incredibly light and refreshing. "Don't judge my bartending skills, though." I carefully measured and poured the ingredients. I examined one of the drinks. It actually looked quite close to Fiona's, but looks could be deceiving. I sipped it. Not bad.

I brought the drinks into the living room and handed one to Fiona. "If you ever want to learn to bartend, let me know. I'll teach you." We quietly sipped our beverages. "I have an idea." She set her glass on the side table and scooted to the edge of her chair. "Hear me out."

Oh boy. I looked at her.

"I think we should go snoop around Kevin's farm." She held her hand up. "I know Barney is doing his detective thing and all, but what if we could nudge the progress along? Just a bit."

I uncrossed my legs and cradled my glass in my lap. "I don't know."

"We won't interfere. Just another set of eyes. We'll only go as far as you're comfortable with."

I was not comfortable at all. But was there any harm? Maybe it could help. I wanted more adventure and living in my life. This wasn't quite what I had in mind. "I guess. But as soon as we see anything, we have to get out of there." I was pretty sure Barney wouldn't approve. But if we happened to find a clue to the murder, how could he complain?

CHAPTER SEVEN

K ayaks were stacked on racks lining the shore. Two paddles inserted into each, ready for the rentals. Early birds were already on the water, dotting the harbor with brightly colored watercrafts. The weather was perfect, a slight breeze brushing through the air, not too warm yet to break out into a sweat. What did one wear for a kayak ride? I needed to be comfortable and not so fancy that it appeared as if we were on a date. I chose a light yellow cotton sleeveless blouse, a tropical patterned skort, and matching pale yellow Converse shoes. Cute but sporty, if I said so myself.

My nerves were already a bit frayed. The mellow splashing of the waves lulled me into a calm. I surveyed the beach in search of Justin. I was a few minutes early, so I walked to the bench next to the rental shack to wait for him. I had never been on a kayak ride. What was I thinking? I was going to make a fool of myself. I shook my head and stood. Maybe this was a bad idea. I looked at my watch. Justin should be here by now. If I left now I could avoid the embarrassment.

Get it together, Tilly.

I plopped onto the bench. This was all part of my new journey. I needed to adjust my mindset to embrace each adventure. I sat back and crossed my legs while the sun warmed my bare skin. I surreptitiously examined my armpit to see if I had already sweated through my blouse. Not yet.

Exiting from the shrubs to my left, Justin arrived. No turning back now. "Tilly, so sorry I'm late," he said.

I looked at my watch. "Actually, you're right on time." I stood and met him.

Justin's brow beaded with moisture. He appeared as anxious as I felt. Well, at least we were in this together.

"Are you OK?" I asked. He was not normally this jittery. Not that I had a lot of firsthand knowledge. But he generally exuded the calmness of the sea.

Justin fiddled with his wallet, turning it over in his hands. "Sure. I was just rushing to get here so you didn't have to wait long." He stepped forward to the rental shack to secure us a kayak.

I pulled money out of my pocket and extended my hand. "Here's my share," I said.

He looked at me and smiled. "Nah, I got this. You can get the next one." He paid the attendant, who pointed to a red kayak at the end of the row. Justin put his wallet away. "Weather cooperated. That's cool," he said.

We headed to our kayak. "Is it ever not this nice in Belle Harbor?" I asked.

"We do have an occasional storm. But overall, the weather doesn't stray far from how it is today," he said. We arrived at the kayak, and Justin removed the paddles and set them to the side. He pushed it about one-third of the way into the water. "Why don't you get in first? Then I'll shove us off and jump in."

I stepped into the kayak with my left leg, facing the shore. He steadied it and my right leg followed. I sat back, waiting for Justin to enter.

He moved to the bow and grabbed the handle. After lifting one end he moved it a bit further into the water. Any more and he would get wet before he could get in. He looked up at me, his sideburns dripping. Hopefully a relaxing trip on the water would allow him to cool off. He picked up the kayak and shoved off to begin our float without jumping in. With outstretched arms, his eyes widened. Unable to stop the momentum of the kayak, he let it go. I drifted farther from the shore. By myself. With no paddles.

"Sorry. Oh, what a dunce." He knocked himself in the head with his fist. "I forget the paddles at the last minute." He looked around.

I floated further from the shore, the waves drawing me out into the harbor.

Justin tried to get another kayak removed from the rope that held the rentals together. He pulled and tugged, unable to free it. He looked around again and scrambled to a pedalboat, dragging it to the water. He looked up. "Hang on. I'll be there in a minute." Just as he jumped into the boat to shove off, he said, "Arghhh," and got out. He raced to gather the two kayak paddles and reentered the pedal boat. Now on the water, he peddled like a madman, pumping his legs as fast as they would go.

I put my hands to the sides of my mouth and hollered, "I'm fine. Don't worry."

He gripped each side of the pedal boat and continued his furious peddling, now close enough to say, "Tilly, I can't believe I did that. I don't know where my head was at. Hopefully you don't think I'm a total birdbrain and you'll give me another chance."

He maneuvered the pedal boat to the side of the kayak and handed me a paddle. "Why don't you take one just in case?"

I tucked the paddle to the side of my seat.

"Grab a hold of this one and I'll tow you in." Justin's T-shirt was now completely pitted out. That poor guy.

I grabbed the end of the second paddle. "Justin?"

He tipped his head up, frowning.

"It's really OK. Think of the story we'll have to tell."

He sat back and took a deep breath. "Thank you for being such a good sport." He took the other end of the paddle I held, turned, and began peddling us back to shore.

I certainly got a kayak ride. Just not exactly as planned. Justin let go of the paddle just as his boat hit the sand. He jumped out, quickly turned, and grabbed the handle of the kayak to pull it onto shore. We reversed the previous steps, and I exited the kayak. He pulled the kayak all the way onto shore and bent over, hands on his knees.

"Are you OK?" I asked, placing my hand on his clammy back. He had quite the workout to rescue me.

"I'm just so embarrassed at my blunder." He straightened up.

"Forget it. I did get my kayak ride, after all," I said.

"Nope, I owe you a real one. With paddles next time." He walked over to the pedal boat to drag it fully onto the shore. He hunched over the side and pulled out a pair of shoes. Converse, dark gray. "These are just like yours. Except they stink to high heaven. I must have been so distracted that I didn't see them when I got in. Or smell them."

Even ten feet away, the odor of the shoes assaulted my nose. I put my hand over it and pointed to the rental shack. "Maybe they have a lost and found."

Justin held the shoes at arm's length, and I followed him from a distance. He chatted with the attendant and dropped the shoes to the side of the shack. He turned and pulled at the front of his T-shirt, which was plastered to his skin, to cool off.

"Even though it didn't go as planned, I had fun. And we'll give it another try," I said. "I should be going. I'm making some treats for Uncle Jack's poker game tonight."

"It's a da—" he started. "It's a deal." His face reddened. He turned, waved, and disappeared down the same pathway he had arrived.

CHAPTER EIGHT

The house on the hill. That's how I had known Uncle Frank and Jack's home from all of my summer visits when I was younger. The view made you feel like you were on top of the world. I would sit on the deck, overlooking the expanse of the ocean, and daydream about possibilities for my life. Some of my fondest memories were conversations with my uncles encouraging me to follow my dreams. I even had visions of living in one of the cottages that were lower down the hill. Never in my wildest imagination did I think it would become a reality.

I entered the front door with my two boxes of surprise treats. I had to sneak around so that Uncle Jack hadn't gotten a preview of what I made. It would either be a resounding success or a total flop. I stopped in the middle of the kitchen, gazing ahead at the wall of windows. The white foam of the waves pounded the shore. The horizon turned a shade of light orange as the sun descended into the far reaches of the ocean.

I called out, "Uncle Jack." I set my boxes on the kitchen counter and continued on to the deck. I stood there grasping the railing, absorbing the moment. This was real. This was my life now.

"Hey sweetheart," Uncle Jack said and joined me at the railing.

I looked up at his sun-weathered face. "Thank you," I said. My new life was becoming everything I had dreamed of. With Uncle Jack's encouragement, my bakery was taking off. I owed him a debt of gratitude for always believing in me.

He took my hand in his and patted it. "It's all you, girl. I'm just along for the ride." He returned through the sliding glass doors to the dining room, which was actually an extension of the kitchen. The poker table held stacks of cards and multi-colored chips. Uncle Jack entered the kitchen, heading for my secret box.

"Don't you dare," I said and rushed inside. I reached in front of him and pushed the boxes further back on the counter. "Wait until everyone gets here."

The back of his hand brushed my cheek. "You got some sun today," he said.

It was what he didn't say that I knew he hinted at. I laughed and led him from the kitchen and the temptation. "Yes, Justin and I went on a kayak ride. At least we tried to." I moved to the living area and sat in an overstuffed chair angled toward the large window. "You'll have to ask him about it."

"Well, that's mysterious," he said and joined me in the matching chair.

"More like hilarious. At least by the time you talk to him, I hope he thinks of it that way," I said.

I stood and eased over to the wall of photos. Family memories covered the entire surface. The one that caught my eye was of Uncle Jack and Frank at the opening of Checkered Past Antiques. It must have been taken at least forty years prior.

"Someday, the legacy could be yours. No pressure, but think about it," Uncle Jack said. "Frank and I talked about it. We would love nothing more than to pass this on to you."

I turned and smiled. A loud pounding on the front door startled us from the walk down memory lane.

"Those turds. Never ones for a subtle entrance." Uncle Jack retraced his steps through the kitchen to let in the rowdy crowd. I was hot on his heels so he didn't take the opportunity to sneak a peek. He opened the door and Barney, Micky, and Gary entered, fully loaded with beer, chips, and pepperoni sticks.

"Tilly, what a pleasure. Didn't expect to see you," Barney said. The group filed in and deposited their goods on the kitchen counter. Barney gave me a peck on the cheek.

"I brought some sweets. Though looking at the haul you guys brought, I should have offered fruits or vegetables," I said.

The guys made their way to the poker table and each took a seat. "Let's get this party started," Gary said. "Tilly, you joining us?"

I stood at the edge of the table and laughed. "No, I don't want to intrude. Plus, I don't really know how to play."

They were all seated now, ready to kick off. Uncle Jack already had a deck of cards in his hand, ready to deal. "You couldn't be any worse than Barney. Maybe his excuse is that he's been distracted lately. And not from the murder investigation." Unkie grinned widely and stared at his friend.

"How is Florence?" Micky asked.

They each scooped up the cards Uncle Jack dealt.

"She's fine. And you all could do with the culture she's just trying to bring to this town." Barney firmly pushed a stack of chips to the center of the table. "Are we going to chitchat or get down to business?" The other three smirked and took the hint. Subject closed.

I returned to the deck and closed the screen door. I hoped when I was that age I had a strong friend group like Unkie did. Despite the jousting, they were true blue to each other.

"Speaking of business," Gary started. The sound of cards and chips hitting the table continued.

"It's a head scratcher," Barney said. Talk had turned to his murder investigation. My ears perked up, and I was hopeful I would hear some news to share with Fiona and could avoid our snooping outing.

"All I know is now that he's gone, that tainted water has stopped flowing onto my property," Gary said.

The poker sounds halted. "What do you mean?" Barney asked.

"Kevin's irrigation system was contaminating my well from the pig poop," Gary said. "We finally figure out why we'd all been sick."

"Gary, play and talk at the same time, or stop talking," Micky said.

That promptly resumed the game.

"I never knew that," Barney said.

Maybe my cookies could ease some tension. I headed to the kitchen for one of my boxes.

"Everyone thought Kevin was such a great guy. I think he had a lot of people fooled," Micky interjected.

Poker night turned out to be much more enlightening than I ever imagined. I opened a box and placed the cookies on a large serving platter. I was pretty sure these guys would eat anything, but I was proud of my experiment with the poker-themed cookies.

"This is the first I'm hearing that you guys felt that way," Barney said. The hand must have ended because someone had scooted a pile of chips across the table.

"Yeah, he wanted everyone to think he was this philanthropic businessman. But behind closed doors, he royally screwed you," Micky said.

"Micky!" Uncle Jack admonished.

"Oh, sorry. But with every deal we did, he kept chiseling me down to almost nothing for my profit margin. I had to sever the business relationship before he bankrupted me," Micky said.

Well, that put a damper on the game.

I entered the dining room and presented my cookie tray to the guys. "All right. I'm unveiling my surprise." They all stood. I started laughing so hard the cookies almost slipped off the tray. I set it in the middle of the poker game. "You can sit," I said.

"Tilly, you've outdone yourself!" Barney said. He grabbed a cookie in the shape of a club, frosted black, and took a huge bite. "Mmmm," he murmured and smiled, his lips tinged dark from the frosting.

"Save some for us," Unkie said.

They all reached for a cookie. This was my joy. Baking treats that made people happy. Researching themed sugar cookies provided me with endless ideas for catering events. It would definitely provide me a creative outlet. I had designed four different patterns: rectangle cards decorated as aces; shapes of each of the four suits: club, spade, heart, and diamond; poker chips; and dice.

"I brought two boxes. Eat up," I said.

Micky patted his belly. "Stand back. This thing is going to be expanding quickly at this rate."

"Can I leave you four unsupervised?" I asked and refilled the plate of cookies. "I've got to get up early for my delivery to Joe's."

"I doubt it," Uncle Jack said. He rose and kissed my cheek. "Thank you, Tilly. You're spoiling us."

I held his hand for a second. My heart was full.

CHAPTER NINE

Today was my second official delivery to Mocha Joe's Coffee Shop. I arrived early to bake up the muffins and cupcakes that we had agreed on. My fledgling bakery was off the ground. Joe shared feedback with me that his customers had raved about them. That warmed my heart. My goal now was to ensure consistency as I worked to improve my processes. As the number of orders increased I needed to be efficient in my production.

I sat at the coffee corner in the quiet of the antique store, enjoying my coffee and planning my day. Uncle Jack's birthday was coming up, and I intended to do everything I could to make it special for the man that deserved it.

The early mornings on the beach were magical. With the sun not quite bathing the beach in warmth yet and the tide out, there were few people. It felt like starting every day anew with so many possibilities. When the crowds eventually arrived, the party atmosphere ensued. At all times there was something for everyone. Feeling the freedom and choice I had with my life gave me a peace I hadn't experienced in a long time, if ever. The move to Belle Harbor was a leap of faith. And it hadn't disappointed one bit.

"Ah, I could smell the coffee and sweets from the sidewalk." Uncle Jack arrived at the shop. "If that doesn't increase the traffic for the antique business, I don't know what would."

I raised from my chair, grabbed the carafe, and poured him a steaming cup. "You guys must have had a late night, Unkie," I said. I retrieved a muffin and a cupcake I had set aside from Joe's order. "This should perk you up." I handed him the plate. I refilled my cup and joined him.

He munched a huge bite of the cupcake and closed his eyes. "That hits the spot. Yeah, it got pretty competitive after you left."

"How long have you been hosting your poker game?" I asked.

He jammed the remaining cupcake into his mouth and followed it with a swig of coffee. "It's been quite a few years."

"Those were some stories Gary and Micky had about Kevin," I said. "The more I hear, the more it sounds like people didn't really like him."

"Yeah, they've been grousing about him off and on over the years. I usually don't pay much mind to it. Just yapping during poker time," he said. He picked up the muffin and examined it from all sides. "I don't know how you do it. Making something healthy taste so good." He dove into the muffin and chased it with more coffee.

"Unkie?" I started. I didn't want to create a rift with his friends. But the thoughts about those two niggled my brain all night. Someone killed Kevin. And sometimes the killer hid in plain sight. Could it be one of those two who were friends with the chief of police? Would they have teamed up to take out someone who had threatened the safety of their family and business?

Uncle Jack looked at me.

"I don't know how to say this," I said.

His cheeks drooped and he sat still.

"Do you think Gary or Micky had anything to do with Kevin's death?" There. I said it. I just couldn't shake the thought that there was more than met the eye.

He vigorously shook his head. "No way."

"No way, what?" Barney arrived and made his way back to the coffee corner.

Uncle Jack rose and got Barney a cup of coffee. They both sat. "You've known Mick and Gary as long as I have. Now, I know they had a beef with Kevin. But killers?" He looked at Barney.

Barney's head bowed as he stared at his cup. "They regularly spouted off about Kevin, but I just can't see it."

"I'm just asking the questions," I said. "I'm not accusing them of anything."

"Yeah," Barney said and took a drink. "It pains me, but I do have to look into every possibility. I really can't say much more right now."

Uncle Jack swung his head toward me, eyes wide. This development would devastate him if one of his friends was a murderer. We needed to let Barney do his job and see this to its natural conclusion.

I shivered, more to shake the sinking feeling than from any chill in the air.

"I think we need to focus on a happier topic," I said. I pointed at Uncle Jack. "I'm planning a birthday bash for this guy. Unkie, do you have any special requests?"

He shook his head. "I love having you here, Tilly. Don't go crazy. You've got enough to do with your business."

"I've got some ideas I think you'll love. And you deserve to be spoiled."

"I agree, Tilly. And I'll help however I can," Barney said.

A crash from the opposite side of the room startled us all out of our seats. We stood and, in unison, proceeded to investigate. In a pile of antiques on a table against the wall, two little eyes peeked out.

"I should have known," Uncle Jack said. "Come here, you little squirt." Unkie reached in to extract Willie without toppling everything on the table. He pulled him out and cradled him, a loud purr following. "He burrowed himself right in between this stash of bottles."

I retrieved one of the dusty and weathered bottles. "It says Jefferson Distillery." I looked at Uncle Jack. "Do you remember if these came in at the same time as the typewriter from that estate sale?"

"That would make sense. But I don't exactly remember. I'd have the paperwork somewhere," he said, continuing to generate a loud purr from the cat.

I picked up another bottle and wiped the label to clearly confirm it was from the Jefferson Distillery. I looked at Barney. "Forgive my amateur sleuthing, but do you think these might have something to do with Kevin's murder?" I quickly put the bottles back on the table and wiped my hands on my shorts, more to rid myself of any connection to that horrid thought than to clear them of the dust.

"I'm not ruling anything out right now. Jack, if you could get me a box, I should probably take these in for potential evidence," Barney said.

I stepped away from the table. "I'll go get a box," I said and rubbed my arms to smooth over the goosebumps. "Here you go." I put the box on the floor next to the table.

"Willie, as much of a stinker as you can be, you might have just helped the case along," Barney said. He retrieved all of the bottles he could find and filled the box. "Jack, if you could do me a favor and look for more. Let me know what you find."

"Sure thing. You heading out so soon?" Uncle Jack asked and put Willie on the floor to scoot away to his hiding spot.

"Yep. Going next door to pick up my book for the book club," Barney said, daring Uncle Jack to tease him.

Right on cue. "What a nerd. You crack me up. I hope you enjoy," Uncle Jack said.

Barney picked up the box of bottles. "Florence thought I might enjoy *Crime and Punishment*. That's our first book." He turned and left the shop.

"I just like to tease him about behaving like a love-struck teenager. But I am happy for him," Uncle Jack said.

I wondered if he was envious of the relationship, wishing he had a love in his life. If so, I might just have to accept the mission to make it happen.

CHAPTER TEN

F iona and I rolled to a quiet stop in her VW bug. My pulse pounded in my ears. I considered whether I should have dressed in all black for our excursion. My amateur sleuthing skills might just get me in trouble. Thankfully I had packed flashlights, as the dark of the country road hid our arrival. She parked her car on a wide part of the road that led to the driveway of the farm. Fiona had donned a black beanie and dressed dark from head to toe, including shoes. This didn't appear to be her first time sneaking around. I wasn't sure I wanted to know about her previous experience.

She pointed. "I think we can go down the driveway for a bit. We have to stay on the side where there's dirt so we don't crunch the gravel. We might have to cut through the trees about halfway down."

How in the world did she know those details about the lay of the land? I looked at her. "Maybe we should rethink this. It doesn't feel right to sneak around on someone's property." The night air had cooled significantly, but I was still sweating bullets. I wanted to help my friend out, but was this the right way to do it?

"It'll be fine. If it looks like anyone sees us, I know a shortcut to get us back to the car." Fiona looked me up and down. "I should have said something before. But your shoes are probably going to get wrecked."

The problem was I didn't have sneaking-onto-a-farm-at-night shoes. My collection consisted of ten different-colored pairs of Converse and my booties for fancier events. I shrugged. "I guess I'm sacrificing them for the cause."

We exited the car and gently clicked the doors closed. Fiona started first and waved me along. The sounds of silence were filled with crickets and the occasional frog in the distance. We continued down the driveway until we got to the cutoff leading to the farm. Once we had the cover of some trees I released a breath I didn't realize I had held.

I whispered, "Fiona."

She stopped.

"Can we make a plan when we get there?" I wanted the exit strategy clearly laid out.

"Oh, yeah. Good idea. When we come to the clearing there will be a big red barn. On the other side of that is the pig pen where Kevin was found. If we stay to the right and sidle up to the barn, nobody from the house will be able to see us." She stared at me.

I nodded. "OK."

"And if lights come on or we hear noise, we'll hide behind the barn." She turned and we worked our way along the path to the clearing. She looked at me again, probably trying to assess my willpower to continue. "You OK?" she asked.

I closed my eyes. We had come this far, might as well go all in. "Yes," I whispered.

The corner of the barn had a spotlight. The space between the edge of the trees and the barn was the only area exposed to the house. We scurried over and stopped to regroup. Fiona grabbed my hand and giggled.

I held a finger up to my mouth to shush her. We tiptoed along the path next to the barn to reach the pig pen. We stopped and scanned the area. So far, so good. Three pigs snored hard in their pen. I was sure we would laugh later about the similarity to the fairytale. For now, we had to remain focused. I only hoped pigs were heavy sleepers. I couldn't imagine what they would do if we startled them awake. All we needed were squealing pigs.

We stepped to the fence housing the pigs and walked the perimeter. Fiona gestured that she was going inside. I grabbed her arm and shook my head. "Let's see what we can find outside first."

"I need to see it from Kevin's perspective," she said.

My chin dropped to my chest. Up 'til now, I was OK. She was pushing our luck. For sure those pigs would wake up, and who knew? Would they charge us in their excitement? I would hate for my new life in Belle Harbor to end with being rammed by swine. I gazed back from the location where we had arrived to make sure I had a clear path for an escape. I gulped.

Fiona lifted the latch on the gate and stepped inside. "You can wait here if you want." She moved to the center of the pen and began rotating to view all angles. I joined her. In one corner was the feed trough. Next to it was a watering trough. The pigs were undisturbed in the little hut laying on some hay. We might just get lucky. Fiona pointed to a stick in a corner. It looked like a handle of a prod that had broken. I looked at her. Was that the murder weapon? Kevin had been hit over the head. Would it have broken the tool?

We continued rotating, taking in every detail of the scene. Nothing else seemed out of place to me. The killer must have sneaked up on Kevin. Or they knew him. That didn't narrow down the list of suspects one bit. I took a step toward the gate, more than ready to leave.

Fiona grabbed my arm and gestured to the side of the pen. I squinted in the direction she pointed. I shook my head, not connecting with her message.

"Footprints that don't look like work boots," she whispered.

Ah, OK. "Can we get out of here now?" Clues or not, I was at the end of my tolerance for investigating.

"Never mind. Those look like your shoes." Fiona led us to the gate—and freedom.

I wasn't sure our adventure netted any new clues. But it sure convinced me I would never make a good criminal. My stomach would take hours to unknot. We quickly left the sleeping pigs and retraced our steps back to the car. We jogged the last leg of our trip and reached the car holding our sides and giggling.

"Fiona, never again. That was stressful," I said. "And I think I'm going to have to burn these smelly clothes and shoes."

She opened the door of the bug and threw me a towel to wipe off. She was prepared. I sat in the passenger seat, removed my shoes, and wrapped them in the towel.

"Tilly, Barney probably already knows this. But that handle might have been part of the murder weapon."

"That's what I thought. But who would come out here and do that?" I asked.

We finished cleaning up and sped away into the night, the windows down to air out the car. The next time I saw Barney I would have to see if he would share progress and find a way to steer the conversation to murder weapon. If it was someone that Kevin knew, who would be angry enough at him to kill him? Was it an argument that went too far? And what was the motive?

CHAPTER ELEVEN

"OK, Willie. If you're going to be a constant fixture here, we've got to properly set you up." Uncle Jack had prepared a bed for Willie behind the checkout counter, but that wasn't enough. Clearly, that cat treated the antique shop as an extension of his home from the apartment upstairs that he shared with Justin.

A small display table nested between a couple of shelves would be perfect. I carefully transferred the antiques to a new location and wheeled the table to the kitchen. I retrieved Willie's bed and placed it on the table, situating the whole thing next to the wall. Willie would have a front row seat to my workspace.

"All right, you spoiled little one, here you go," I said and picked him up. He lifted his head and began purring. "You stay here, though. Can't have cat fur showing up in my pastries. Not good for business."

"What's not good for business?" Unkie's voice boomed from the open door. He held two Mocha Joe's coffee cups and offered one to me.

"Thank you." I nodded my head toward Willie's new perch. "That one." I took a sip of the coffee and closed my eyes. I needed about ten of these to perk me up after last night's excursion with Fiona. "He's been pestering me ever since I whipped up this cream cheese frosting."

Uncle Jack stared at me.

"What?" I took another sip of coffee. I just knew he could see bags protruding from under my eyes, giving away my secret.

"Did you have a late night?" he asked and smiled.

"It's not what you think. It was just Fiona and me hanging out."

I set the coffee to the side and picked up my bowl of frosting. Willie let out a loud yowl. I got a small mixing bowl and placed a teaspoon of frosting in it and tucked it into the corner of Willie's bed. He now had a new bowl. He jammed his face in, practically wearing the bowl like a hat. I resumed icing the three-layer chocolate cake.

"Joe said your muffins and cupcakes are flying off the shelf. Way to go hon," Unkie said.

"Did you go down there to buy my cupcakes?" I looked up at him. "You know I'll make them for you whenever you want."

He scooped another teaspoon of icing for Willie to shush the mewing cat. Justin would wonder why his cat was up all night from the sugar high. "Well, I did have one. But I met Micky for coffee. He's pretty upset about Kevin."

I looked up, my spatula mid-swipe on the cake.

"Don't worry. Micky's a good guy. I don't think he had anything to do with Kevin's death." Uncle Jack got a new spoon and sneaked a taste of the frosting. "Mmmm."

"You don't think?" I looked down, and my spatula had stabbed the cake. I withdrew it and scooped some frosting to repair the break.

"Tilly, let Barney do his job. And you keep making these incredible creations."

I smiled. "This is for you. I made two samples of cake for you to choose for your birthday party."

He looked at the end of the counter as I pointed to a covered plate.

"I made carrot cake, and this is a classic chocolate that will be covered in sprinkles."

He laughed. "Why do you keep trying to sneak vegetables into the sweets? That's just not right." He reached in for another sample of the frosting.

I playfully slapped his hand. "No double-dipping. And you can't even taste them. They add a depth of flavor and moisture too."

"Well, not because of the vegetables, but you had me at sprinkles with this one. That sounds more like me," he said.

"Sprinkles it is. And lots of them," I said.

Unkie and I turned our heads at the sound of footsteps. Barney approached us with his police hat tucked under his arm. "Jack, do you ever work anymore now that you have a bakery in the corner of your store?"

"You old fart. I'll have you know this bakery has more than doubled my business. Might have to give Tilly a cut of the profits," Uncle Jack said. "Enough about me. I don't think I've ever seen you visit as much as you have until that bookstore opened next door."

I continued frosting the cake as Willie beckoned for more samples and Unkie and Barney traded jabs.

"How was the book club?" Uncle Jack inquired.

Barney's typically stoic demeanor immediately transformed into flustered, fidgeting hands. "Excellent. A nice change of pace from the good ole boys club. Florence knows how to do it right," he said. "I'd invite you, but I think you'd just goof off the whole time."

"Yeah, you're probably right. Say, I had coffee with Mick this morning. He's pretty nervous about being considered a suspect. What gives?" Uncle Jack asked.

"I know. But it can't be helped. He certainly had a motive. That bad business deal with Kevin last year sent him reeling from the financial losses. He lost his house. They had to move in with his mom."

"But that don't make a killer." Uncle Jack held a hand up. "I know. You've told me a thousand times. People stay on the suspect list until you have a compelling reason to remove them."

"I wish I was farther along so I could ease some people's minds." Barney looked around the store and leaned in. "I think the killer surprised Kevin when he was feeding his pigs. But I think he knew who it was. I can't say more than that." Barney stepped back.

Goosebumps raised on my entire body. Fiona and I were literally at the nexus of the scene of the crime last night. It creeped me out to envision Kevin's last minutes and what might have happened. I rotated the cake on the little round table and applied the finishing touches. I scooted the carrot cake to the center of the counter and lifted the cover, then retrieved two plates and forks.

"Could I trust you two to sample the cakes and decide which will be the winner for the birthday bash?" I asked.

Barney's eyes lit up. "All day long," he said, grabbing a knife to begin slicing and serving. "Carrot is my favorite."

"That figures," Unkie said and elbowed Barney. "I already chose the chocolate with sprinkles. You can keep the one with veggies."

Resuming his yowl, Willie chimed in for more frosting. I rolled my eyes. What a hoot these three were.

"You heading out?" Uncle Jack asked with his mouth full of carrot cake.

Don't like vegetables in desserts? I snickered. Put enough sugar in anything, and Unkie would eat it. "I thought I'd go back and reserve a kayak for Justin and me since our first outing was kind of a disaster."

"You never did tell me what happened," Uncle Jack said and inhaled the rest of the carrot cake slice.

"That's not for me to tell." I untied my apron and put it on the hook. I grabbed my backpack and helmet. "Don't eat that whole thing, you'll ruin your dinner. I don't want to come back here and find you both splayed on the floor in a sugar coma." I shook my head. Just like a couple of teenage boys.

CHAPTER TWELVE

I didn't like to lie to Unkie. Truthfully, I was headed to the kayak rental, but not only to book one for another outing with Justin. I was really bothered by those shoes he found in the paddle boat. There was something about them being there that day that just didn't sit right. I puttered out to the street on my moped, the sun warming my face. I zoomed past the rows of cottages lining the street, the little places similar to mine.

The kayak rental shop was at the far end of the harbor, near the lighthouse. I slowed down and turned into the entrance, pulling into a parking spot. I removed my helmet and shook out my hair. I was due for another tint, but not sure what color to go with this time. I loved the blue, but it was fading into my natural brown. I felt bold enough to go for a brighter shade. Coloring my hair like Grandma Luna had done for herself somehow made me feel closer to her.

I approached the kayak rental shack, glad to see it was the same guy working as it was the other day Justin and I came. I gulped and stopped. Maybe this was a dumb idea. What if he wouldn't tell me? What if he got mad at me? I closed my eyes and clenched my fists, steeling my nerves. *OK, let's do this.* I pasted a smile on my face and said, "Hello."

The guy looked up from his phone and hopped off the stool. "Hey." He squinted at me. "Weren't you here the other day? I'd remember that hair anywhere."

I inhaled, and upon my exhale, said, "I have a question."

He furrowed his brows. "OK."

"Can you tell me who rented the paddle boat before we used it the other day?" I unclenched my hands and wiggled my fingers.

He stepped back and shook his head, pulling the registration book away from me. "Nah, can't do that."

I shrugged. "Well, OK. How about—"

"But if you wanted to reserve a kayak, you would need to write your name in the registration book." He stared at me.

Message received. "Yes, I want to reserve a kayak for this weekend." He was really going to let me look at the book.

"What time?" He turned the book to face me and handed me a pen.

"Well, uh," I started and tapped the pen on my chin. I hadn't cleared this with Justin, but there was no stopping me now. "I think ten should work." My hand jostled the last of my entry. I looked up. "Do I owe you anything today?" I hoped he hadn't seen my nervous gesture.

He stared, probably thinking I was a loon, wondering if I could be trusted with a kayak rental. "Nope, you're good. See you Saturday."

I turned and sped away, at the last minute yelling over my shoulder, "Thank you."

My heart raced. I did it. This detective stuff wasn't for the faint of heart. I returned to my moped and headed to my next errand. I was beside myself with excitement about planning Unkie's birthday party. The wharf was located at the opposite end of town from the kayak rental. This moped was a genius purchase idea from Uncle Jack. Getting around this way was fun and simple. Thankfully, the machine hadn't pooped out after the initial problems, and my confidence riding it increased each time. I sat tall, working my way to the wharf parking lot. On my right side a woman was handing out cotton candy samples, and she handed me one as I drove by. I stopped the moped and took a bite of the sweet puff. Hmmm, that gave me some ideas for pastry flavors. That's something I could work with.

I headed down the wharf to the cruise rental office. The sun sparkled on the rotating Ferris wheel, laughter coming from the riders. Happy sounds. I shaded my eyes. About halfway down the pier, I spotted a person that looked like Micky seated with another man at an outdoor cafe table. I slowed my pace to study him. The man had a baseball cap tipped to the side of his head, partially obscuring his face. I couldn't miss that beard. And his tie-dyed shirt was awfully similar to the one he wore at poker the other day. I was sure that was him. He seemed to be trying to hide from observation.

I quickly entered the cruise ship office, shaking my head. What was up with that?

"I see you met Cristie," the woman said and pointed to my hand that held the cotton candy.

I smiled. "That made my day."

"She's opening a new shop and giving out samples," the woman said. She wore a navy, collared, short-sleeved shirt with an anchor on the arm and white shorts.

"It's really good. I'd like to see about a rental for my uncle's birthday party."

"Great," she said. "Did you have something in mind?"

"Well, I'm new in town. There will be about ten of us. What do you suggest?"

The woman got a brochure and placed it on the counter. "We actually have a super fun cruise for smaller groups on our vintage Thomas International school bus. It's been refurbished and made to float."

I looked at the brochure. "That couldn't be more perfect! My uncle is Jack Steele, owner of Checkered Past Antiques. I'm Tilly." I reached my non-sticky hand across the counter to shake.

"Nice to meet you. I'm Ruthie," the woman said, stepping to my side of the counter. "If you want, we can take a quick look," she offered.

I looked at the door, contemplating. "I think it will be fine. Do I need to put down a deposit?" I continued looking at the door, unable to get the scene with Micky out of my head.

"Yes. Ten percent will hold it," she said. "We also have packages of party supplies that you can add. Would you like to see those?" She reached for a notebook on the end of the counter.

"Umm." Where had my manners gone? "I'm sorry. I have a lot on my mind. I'm going to supply everything. Thank you, though." I paid the deposit and wandered from the office, mindlessly finishing my cotton candy sample. I retraced my steps to the moped and set my backpack on the ground, pulling out my phone. She would know what to do about Micky.

I dialed Fiona's number. Ugh. Voicemail. She was a busy business owner, so what did I expect? "Fiona, it's Tilly. I'm not sure how to say this." I looked up to see if anyone else was nearby. "I just saw Uncle Jack's friend Micky at the wharf. He was with another guy, and I don't know. It just seemed sketchy. I'm sure it's nothing. But call me back when you get this." I paused before the message cut me off. "Can't wait for game night tomorrow. If I don't talk to you before, I'll see you then."

I hung up and sat on my moped, watching the growing crowd head toward the Ferris wheel. I looked at the top of it. I bet you could see the whole town from there.

CHAPTER THIRTEEN

U ncle Jack had finally relented and let me help him organize some of the antiques into more presentable displays. After the incident with the broken vase he had knocked onto the floor, he admitted he could use some help. We had plowed through about half of the store today, and I had to say, it looked incredible. A few regular customers had loaded up on purchases, more than ever before. After they left the shop, Unkie winked at me, approval for a job well done. My specialty was order.

I was glad to be in a routine of making the cupcakes and muffins for Mocha Joe's Coffee Shop, but that was not going to sustain me in business. I needed much bigger orders to make this a viable operation. I'd spotted a party store on my way to the wharf yesterday that I would visit and see if I could forge a partnership. That was bound to be an opportunity to provide goodies for all kinds of celebrations.

I decided on casual clothes for the game night at Fiona's. A graphic print tee with a whimsical lobster, shorts, and my standard Converse shoes, today in neon green. I didn't want any fancier clothes to give Justin an inkling about my feelings, whatever they were.

Every time I entered Fiona's, the energy enveloped me. Tonight was no different. The place was packed. Servers buzzed around for the customers. The bar was full. I hoped I wasn't too late to join in the games.

"Tilly, right on time," Fiona yelled and gestured for me to get closer in toward the bar. "OK, everyone. We're just about to get started. You know the drill. Two teams." She returned to making several drinks, filling the glasses quickly and handing them to a server.

I looked around to see what I was supposed to be doing. Justin started my direction when Anna grabbed his arm and pulled him into the small group forming on the other side of the bar.

"No you don't," Anna said. "You're with me." She glared at me over her shoulder as if to say she won that round. She whipped her head around, her long blonde ponytail smacking Justin in the face.

We were teams of five each. I had no idea how this worked; I just didn't want to make a fool of myself. Fiona reiterated the rules and read the first question. "Henry the eighth introduced which tax in England in 1535?"

"Beard," Anna screamed and raised her hands in victory formation. She turned and gripped Justin in an awkward hug. He pushed her away. How would anyone know that? I felt defeated. There was no way I could help my team.

Fiona continued with nine more questions. "OK, team one"—she glanced down at her paper and pointed toward Justin and Anna—"has eight. Team two has two." She pointed in my direction. "Break time for ten minutes, then we finish up." Anna attempted another hug with Justin, who straight-armed her this time.

Fiona called me into the corner for a little quiet. "Sorry I didn't call back. What are you thinking about Micky? Who was the other guy?"

I shrugged. "Not sure. It might be nothing. But my instincts are telling me otherwise."

"Was it a tall guy, dark hair, mustache?" she asked.

My eyes widened. "Do you know him?"

"I think it might be his new business partner." She furrowed her brow. "I've seen them together too."

"What?" I asked.

"I'm with you. Could be nothing. But maybe we should let Barney know. I just wonder if the two of them together did something to

Kevin for revenge." Fiona looked at her watch and gazed around the bar.

I gasped. One of Uncle Jack's poker buddies. I hoped for my uncle's sake that it wasn't true. But we needed to find out for certain.

"We should get started again. We have a lot of games left," Fiona said and returned to the center of the horseshoe bar. She clapped her hands for attention, and the players resumed their positions.

"Team two, you better get it in gear if you want a chance at winning tonight," Fiona teased.

She began the second half of the game. Several questions in and our team was within one point of team one.

"Come on, losers, I need the money," Anna belted toward her team. She stepped back, red-faced at her outburst, bumping into Justin.

Fiona scowled, holding up the cards for the last two questions. With prize money on the line, the game had turned serious. Truthfully, Anna seemed to be the only one not taking it in stride.

Fiona read the last question. "What is Scooby Doo's full name?"

"I know it." Anna's hand shot up. At this point we all wanted to let her have it and be done. The game had become not so fun anymore. "Scoobert Doo!" She looked around for the adoration from her team. Seeing none, she leapt into Justin's arms and kissed his cheek.

That guy was quite the gentleman to put up with that. I was sure Fiona was contemplating changes to the game to avoid Anna's antics in the future. Seeing a need to rescue Justin, Fiona approached and grabbed his hand, leading him to my side of the bar. Anna continued to high five her teammates, who were attempting to distance themselves from her.

"Maybe next time you can be on my team," Justin said.

I smiled. "Hey, I booked us another kayak ride, if you're game."

"Always. I need to redeem myself. Thanks for doing that." He turned toward Fiona. "I have to go. Thanks for a fun time," he said and left.

Fiona stepped closer to me. "Another date?"

"Stop it. He's just showing me the town. Hey, something else occurred to me." I grabbed Fiona's arm and pulled her in to whisper in her ear. I shared my revised theory. It felt really over the top. If I accused someone who wasn't guilty of killing Kevin, it could ruin their life. But if I was right, I had to follow my gut. Nobody should get away with murder.

"What do you think?" I asked. I nervously shook my hands. If Fiona said go for it, I would.

"I think you need to call Barney."

"I do too." I pulled my phone out of my pocket and looked around the busy bar. Too noisy in here and I didn't want anyone to overhear. I held up the phone. "I'll step outside."

Fiona nodded. "Trust your instincts, Tilly," she said. "We'll start our next round of games when you get back."

I turned and left the crowded bar.

CHAPTER FOURTEEN

The evening air had cooled, splashing my face for a reality wake-up. I sat on the bench next to the front wall of Fiona's, confirming I was alone. I held the phone in my hands, the number entered. I took a deep breath and pushed the dial button. After two rings Barney answered. There was no turning back now. I put the phone to my ear.

"Hey, Tilly. You calling about the old man's birthday bash plans?" Barney asked.

I smiled.

"Not this time. I have something else for you. It might seem like a crazy idea. But I have to share what I know and let the professional do his work." I stood and walked further from the front door of Fiona's. A few small bonfires dotted the beach from the evening crowd. I forced the words out of my mouth. Once I began, they continued to flow, spilling out my premise for Kevin's murder. Barney was silent the entire time. I held my phone away from my ear and looked to be sure I was still connected. "Barney?"

"I'm here," he said. "I'm making notes."

"I know it's far-fetched. But do you think it's possible?" I asked.

"You'd be surprised how reality is stranger than fiction, hon," he said. "And Tilly?"

He waited for me to answer. "Yes?"

"Don't say anything. I think you're on the right track," Barney said.

I shuddered. Fiona stuck her head outside and looked up and down the sidewalk. She waved at me. I nodded and held up a finger, signaling I was almost done.

"You don't have to worry. I'll take it from here," Barney said.

"Thank you. And yes, I've got plans in the works for Unkie's party," I said, ending the call on a happy note.

I was so pumped for the shindig, to be able to treat Uncle Jack for all of the kindness and love he showed me.

I gulped in the cool, clear air before returning inside. The dinner crowd had thinned a bit, and the remaining customers were primarily at the bar, ready for round two of games.

Fiona held two hula hoops in her hand. She instructed the two teams on the rules of the game. It was a head-to-head competition. The person on the team to hula longer than the other would get a point. Two rounds.

She finished her explanation, which promoted a response from Anna. "Boo. This is lame. Let's do more trivia."

Anna's team glared at her. I was pretty sure that outburst might just get her banned from game night. Fiona intended for fun, but the competition for the prize was making it too serious.

Anna stepped forward and grabbed a hoop. "Well, let's get on with it." She looked at me, daring me to take her on.

Fiona deliberately handed the hoop to someone else on my team. I needed to thank her later for helping me avoid that direct confrontation.

"OK. As soon as the hoop hits the floor, you're out," Fiona advised.

We all stepped back and the two hula contestants began on Fiona's "ready, set, go." Anna had taken the lead, smoothly swirling the hoop around her waist. Her opponent wildly swiveled his hips, trying to keep the hoop in flight, but to no avail.

Anna raised her hands in victory, letting the hoop drop to the floor. As she picked it up to hand it to the next in line, I noticed she had shoes identical to mine. Not a big deal. A lot of people liked Converse brand shoes. But the kicker was the rest of her outfit was identical to the one I wore the other day at the beach with Justin. I shivered. This was more than coincidence. It creeped me out.

I took a seat at the bar to wait my turn, nursing another paloma cocktail. Anna plopped into the chair next to me. I fixed my eyes on the next hula duo.

"Whew, that's a workout," Anna said.

I glanced down as I sipped my beverage. "Nice shoes." I couldn't help myself. "Just like mine." I stuck my leg out for her to see.

"Oh, you're copying me," she said and straightened in her seat.

"Yours look pretty new," I said. I hopped off the chair and grabbed the hula hoop to take my turn. "Did those replace the stinky pair from the pig pen?"

Her eyes widened. She reached for her drink and took a long swig, wiping her mouth with the back of her hand. "I've had these forever. I'm just now wearing them."

"Except," I started. From the corner of my eye, I spotted Barney enter the doorway. He stepped to the side and scanned the room. "You left your other pair behind in the paddle boat." I moved to the center of the room to begin the next round of hooping.

Anna slipped off the bar stool. "You don't know what you're talking about. You think you can come to this town and just take over? With your stupid little cupcakes that aren't even very good."

I held the hoop, ready to begin. Her jab hurt my ego a bit. I was still learning the baking thing, but people told me they liked my cupcakes.

Anna continued slinking toward the door.

"Tilly," Fiona said. I looked at her, ready to begin hooping. I was under no illusion that I would be any good, ready to hand the victory over to my opponent. Fiona tilted her head toward Anna. Message received.

I removed the hoop and rushed toward Anna, looping it over her shoulders, capturing her in place. She squirmed to get loose, stomping on my shoes. I quickly moved my foot and she lost her balance. Barney stepped forward and took the hoop from me. "Tilly, I think you've just invented a new police tactic. Nice work," he said.

I grinned. My attempted doppelganger hung her head and sobbed. "It's not fair," she said as she sniffled.

Barney let the hoop drop and pulled cuffs from his belt. "Anna Bridges. You are under the arrest for the murder of Kevin Packton," Barney finished reciting her Miranda rights.

"You'll pay for this, Tilly," Anna hollered over her shoulder as Barney led her from the bar.

I turned and the room exploded in a round of applause. Shouts of "congratulations," "way to go," "buy that girl another drink" rang out. My hands shook.

Fiona rushed and enveloped me in a huge hug. She held me at arm's length, holding up her hand for a high five. "You are so brave."

I shook my head as she escorted me to a bar stool. "My instincts took over, thankfully. With my energy amped up, I feel like I could whip everyone at this hooping contest." I laughed.

"I think game night is over for now," she said. "Actually, I was considering canceling it all together. Every time Anna came, it got weird and too serious. I'm all about the fun."

"I'm figuring that out," I said.

Fiona gave me a squeeze and returned to bartend. "I think you and I are just getting started, my friend." She set out several glasses and started mixing the cocktails like a pro.

I was pretty sure Unkie would have a lot of questions next time I saw him. Word traveled fast in this town, and no telling how the story would evolve by the time it got to him. He would probably be high fiving me as well.

CHAPTER FIFTEEN

"Thank you, Steven." The grocery delivery boy set the bags of ingredients and supplies on the kitchen counter in the back of Uncle Jack's antique shop. My space was wall-to-wall with baking items. I could barely move to do what I needed. I loved seeing Unkie every day and didn't want to think about my own place yet. I had to find a way to make this work as long as possible. I wasn't ready for that change.

"You're welcome, ma'am," the teenager said and slightly bowed.

How did I get old enough to be a ma'am? I certainly didn't feel that old. But with the events from the last several days, I sure did feel tired. Sleuthing with my new friend Fiona and capturing a murderer sapped my energy. I needed to perk up for Uncle Jack's party. I wanted it to be epic.

I began unpacking the bags.

"Need any help?" Uncle Jack asked.

His business boomed as well. He could actually use the space where he had built my kitchen in his shop to display more antiques if he wanted. It warmed my heart that he traded that for having me here.

I chuckled.

"What? My organization is getting better," he said and extracted the remainder of the groceries and folded the paper bags.

I held up a hand. "You're right." I looked around. Since I had arrived in town, Unkie had significantly improved the layout of the store. Almost every customer who shopped now bought something. He was a bit stubborn at first to make any changes. He and his brother Frank had run the store for decades and did well. I think the idea to change ultimately became his. Then there was no stopping him.

"Til, you're so busy. You don't have to worry about my birthday. We can just go to Fiona's." He looked at me.

Uncle Jack was a people person. No way was I letting his birthday celebration be that tame.

"That ship has sailed, so to speak," I said. Booking that cruise was a brilliant stroke, if I don't say so myself.

"If you're sure." His jowls drooped. He had gotten all serious on me, which was unlike him.

I rounded the kitchen counter and grabbed one of his hands in mine. I peered into his eyes. "You deserve this and more. Let me do it for you." I returned his glare. "It's settled. So I have the guest list drafted. I'm assuming poker buddies for sure."

"Yep. Although, I don't know if we can invite Barney without Florence. Seems they are getting along quite well." Uncle Jack smirked. He really loved to tease his friend, and this gave him a whole new line for the kidding.

"The more the merrier," I said. "But..." I started. I busied myself with some sugar cookies cutters. "Are you sure about Micky? I mean, I know he didn't kill Kevin. But his behavior at the wharf really bothered me."

Uncle Jack took a couple of cookie cutters and held them up to his eyes like star-shaped glasses. What a goof. Always trying to ease the tension. "It was his brother visiting. The two of them hadn't been on good terms for a long time. Micky's trying to mend the relationship."

"Give me those." I reached for the cutters and returned them to the box. My repertoire of baked items was growing. Getting into frosted sugar cookies was one of my next major steps. I had so many ideas of shape, colors, and designs, and I couldn't wait.

"Tilly, I can't figure out how you suspected Anna of killing Kevin?" Uncle Jack shuffled his feet. He fashioned himself as a good judge of character. He had known Anna when she worked at the moped shop until she had been fired for badmouthing the boss.

"I made an educated guess. Her shoes definitely caught my eye. And Fiona told me about her trying to get hired by Kevin. That her family had owned the Jefferson Distillery that went out of business quite a long time ago. I wonder if she wanted revenge."

Unkie took a step back and put his hand on his heart. I think it hurt him to see a young person go bad. "She must have held a grudge for quite a long time." He shook his head. "Barney said that letter we found in the typewriter led him to an old chest on the Jefferson property. There was another letter in there of a confession of a murder during prohibition of someone that tried to put them out of business."

"Well, and Fiona and I snooped on Kevin's property," I blurted. I had to get it out in the open. I kept my head down, ready for the backlash.

"Tilly!" And there it was.

I slowly lifted my head. "I know, I know. But I don't think I would have put the clues together otherwise," I said.

"You certainly have a streak of your grandma Luna's boldness in you. But it also nicely complements your logical, organized side."

We both whipped our heads around at a yowl coming from the front door. It didn't sound like Willie. We followed the noise, and sure enough, Florence's cat Gwinnie had arrived for a visit. Willie strutted from his bed behind the checkout counter like he was expecting a visitor. The two of them circled each other for a second, then began nuzzling.

I felt like we were watching a show. Willie led Gwinnie to the back of the store, and they disappeared behind the counter. I looked at Uncle Jack, my eyes wide and my hand over my mouth to stifle a laugh.

"Oh boy. Those two really seem to like each other. We should probably return Gwinnie to Florence before she starts to worry." Uncle Jack followed the duo and scooped Gwinnie up. Willie looked at her as if to acknowledge he would see her again soon.

"Yeah, I don't think that's the last time you'll have to do that," I said and followed Uncle Jack.

He exited the store and stopped. "Oh no."

I looked around him and saw a reddish-colored chicken that looked suspiciously like my one from my neighbor enter Florence's Bookstore. We followed the hen.

Florence looked up from the box of books she was unpacking. "What are you doing with my Gwinnie?"

Uncle Jack handed the cat to Florence. "She was visiting Willie. I didn't want you to worry about her. If you are ever looking for her, she's probably next door." He wiped his hand on his shorts to rid them of cat fur.

Florence looked down and took a step back, seeing the chicken in her bookstore. "Well, keep your mangy cat away from my princess." She hugged Gwinnie closer and pointed with a free hand. "And take that chicken with you."

The chicken had found a space in a reading nook between the bookshelves and was perched in the corner.

"Got it," Uncle Jack said. He squeezed between the chair and the wall and hoisted the chicken into his arms. He paused mid-lift and turned to look at me over his shoulder. He grinned widely, his face hidden from Florence. Sure enough, underneath the chicken right next to the table lay an egg.

Uncle Jack scooped up the egg, turned, and sped from the store.

I quickly followed. "Bye Florence." I waved, snickering under my breath. That's all we needed to add to this crazy mix. A rogue chicken who adopted the bookstore as her new laying nest.

Read on for a scrumptious sprinkle cake, bookstore chickens, and Tilly seeing double in ***Birthday Cake and Burglary***

BIRTHDAY CAKE AND BURGLARY

A Belle Harbor Cozy Mystery

Book 3

CHAPTER ONE

T he midday sun bathed my bare skin in warmth like a cozy blanket. On a short break from baking, I decided to take a spin on the Ferris wheel at the end of the wharf. As the wheel stopped to load passengers, I sat in the carriage at the top with a view of the entire Belle Harbor waterfront. The blue sky was clear as a bell. The only remnants from the early morning storm were the waves crashing loudly against the shore. The thunder had awakened me last night and seemed to greatly disturb my neighbor's chickens. I didn't know if that was good or bad for egg production.

The carriage began to sway as the wheel resumed turning to allow the next set of passengers to board. I panned the skyline, surveying the place that had become my home. Uncle Jack's Checkered Past Antiques shop was nestled among other quaint locations along the boardwalk. He and Uncle Frank had run that business for over forty years. It was a blessing beyond measure that he had taken me in and carved out a little space for my baking kitchen. My fledgling dream to open my own bakery like my Grandma Luna was coming true because of him and his belief in me.

The wheel jostled, bringing me back to the present. I literally felt on top of the world and was learning to love life again. My move away from Boston—and my cheating ex—was the initial step in liberating the new me. I was choosing myself for probably the first time in my life. The pain of my divorce ran deep. To say I was surprised by the series of events that led to the separation would be an understatement. It hadn't ever occurred to me that I wouldn't be married to the man who at one time had been the love of my life. The therapy of the beach and the support of Uncle Jack were the salve for my pain.

The beach teemed with vacationers and locals soaking up the tropical atmosphere. The palm trees waved in the distance, beckoning all to partake in the ambiance. I breathed in the fresh salt air, watching the kids build their sandcastles. One little boy dug a hole that filled with water from the encroaching waves. He splashed his sister and a water fight ensued with shrieks of pure joy.

As I gazed further down the beach to my left, an unnatural motion caught my eye. Uncle Jack told me the top of the old lighthouse had been transformed into a small restaurant. Next to the other side of the fixture, a large object fell from the railing of the nearby trail. I rubbed my eyes and squinted. I shaded the sun with my hands and stretched my neck. The wobbling of the carriage made it hard to focus on a destination that far away. It couldn't be. At least I hoped it wasn't so.

The shorebirds were quite active after the storm had passed through. I must have seen them hugging the shore and the rocks below the lighthouse. I turned away, allowing my eyes to rest. I twisted back and scooted to the edge of the carriage and stared. Now there was no doubt. Someone had fallen from the upper ledge. A body was sprawled on the sand—and they weren't moving. I pulled out my phone to use the zoom on the camera to get a better look. It appeared to be a woman with shoulder length brown hair, a blue shirt, and grayish pants. Still no movement. I looked up from where she had fallen but didn't see anyone else nearby. There was nobody to help her.

I was four stops away from getting off the ride. What could I do? The lighthouse wasn't far from Fiona's bar at the far end of the boardwalk. Perhaps I could call her to take a quick look. The wheel continued stopping and starting for passenger loading and disembarking. I looked toward the fallen woman another time, hoping with each glance that I would see her push herself up. Instead, I spotted what appeared to be a large man in a T-shirt and shorts running from the same location. A baseball cap covered some of his face, but not the brown beard and glasses. He skirted the base of the lighthouse and disappeared down a path away from the boardwalk toward Main Street.

I peered over the side of my carriage, now one stop away from the bottom. I briefly contemplated jumping out to go investigate the body. My muscles tensed, ready to spring forth when the door was opened.

"Thank you for coming," the young ride attendant said with a big smile.

I returned the gesture and took several steps, glancing around as I called Fiona. She was located a lot closer to the lighthouse and could get to the lady much quicker than I could. On ground level, the body was obscured from my view by the rocks and shrubs at the bottom of the cliff. With every breath I hoped the lady's head would pop up above the border. I began walking that direction waiting Fiona's answer, navigating between the many families enjoying their time.

"Hey girl," I heard from the other end of the telephone connection. Fiona's exuberance was contagious. She had late nights working at the bar, but that never kept her from being extremely chipper first thing in the morning. Likely Mocha Joe's extra-large coffees contributed to her level of energy. "What's up?"

"Fiona," I started but second-guessed myself. "It's probably nothing." I paused.

"Where are you?" she asked.

I stopped and looked back at the Ferris wheel. "I'm halfway between the Ferris wheel and the lighthouse." I stood on my toes to see if I could see the body. Not yet. "This is going to sound outrageous. I'm pretty sure I saw someone fall from the cliff next to the lighthouse." I trudged through the thick sand, sweat now dripping from my brow.

"You mean at the Belle Harbor Beach Park? Are you sure?" she asked.

"I'm on my way there now. Can you meet me?" I asked, stopping to catch my breath.

"Maybe it was a branch or something that slipped loose from all of the rain last night," she said. "I'm walking that direction."

"No, I saw a person," I said. "Nobody else must have seen it. They're all immersed in their own business." Beach goers were reading, building sandcastles, on their phones, laying on towels soaking up sun, all in their own world. "Oh, I hope she's OK. Fiona we have to help her."

"I can see you now. Pink shirt, right?" Fiona waved.

"Yes," I said and waved back, beginning a jog. I ran the final hundred yards to Fiona's side.

She hugged my clammy body and took my hand, leading me in the direction I pointed.

"Stacy is covering for me," Fiona said, answering my unasked question. She pulled me along as we reached the base of the lighthouse. We circled the building to the other side where the beach park was situated. A steep trail ascended from the beach to the location where I had seen the woman fall from. Fiona looked at me.

I stopped and pointed. A broken rail from the fence lay on the ground.

CHAPTER TWO

We turned toward the direction of the body. I couldn't see over the steep pile of rocks to the unknown state of the woman on the other side. My stomach churned with the reality that she was probably dead. We stepped to the edge of the rock pile and began our trek over the mound. I crawled, staying low, steadying my feet with each step. My foot slipped on a loose boulder and my knee slammed into it, leaving a bright pink scrape. I kept my head down, avoiding the inevitable reality. Fiona and I carried on to the top of the pile. I stopped and grabbed Fiona's hand again, kneeling as we surveyed the scene.

Splayed on the sand in front of us, the woman remained immobile. I squinted to see if there was any movement from breathing. The wind continued its strong gusts in the aftermath of the storm. Her shirt ruffled slightly with what I hoped was her breath.

"Oh no. That's Poppy," Fiona said. She carefully picked her way over the remaining rocks and descended to the sand on the other side of the pile. Looking over her shoulder at me she continued, "She's the owner of the pizza parlor." Fiona peered at the cliff above. "I wonder if she lost her balance."

I navigated over the remaining rocks to Fiona's side. "I'm so sorry, Fiona," I said and put my arm around her shoulder.

She shook her head. "I didn't think it was this bad."

The waves to our left inched closer to us and Poppy. The tide encroached on the sand, depositing foam several feet from us. Poppy lay face down. Her brown hair fanned out around her head. Her arms and legs stretched out like she was making a snow angel.

"What do you mean?" I asked, moving Fiona's hair away from her face.

"I just hope she didn't jump to her death."

My hand flew to my mouth, and I gasped. Goosebumps populated my arms, making me shiver.

"Fiona, why would you say that?" I asked. I crouched over Poppy's body, reaching my arm toward her neck. I stuck my pointer finger out and placed it on her skin to see if there was any life. I looked up at Fiona. She closed her eyes. I stood and grabbed my phone from my back pocket. We needed to get the police here soon to investigate before the sea washed away the evidence.

Fiona turned and moved toward the rock pile, sitting on a flat boulder and stretching out her legs. Her head drooped. "I don't want to speak ill of the dead. She was such a nice lady."

I joined Fiona on the rocks, fumbling with my phone, as the relentless motion of the waves seeped further toward the shore.

Fiona continued, "She'd been coming to the bar more often and was drinking quite a bit the last couple of months." She sniffled and wiped her nose with the back of her hand, then gazed toward Poppy, stood, and looked down at me. "I think her business was doing well. But her personal life was in the toilet." She began to pace along the pile of rocks.

I stood and took a deep breath. I held out my phone and said, "I need to call Barney." I moved away from Fiona to a location closer to the cliff, partly to get out of the wind noise and also out of earshot from Fiona. I turned my back toward her and dialed the police department. In my gut I didn't think Poppy had jumped or accidentally fallen either. I didn't know her, but something didn't sit right about the whole thing. I couldn't get the image of that guy running from the location out of my head. I closed my eyes to burn those details into my memory so I could more effectively recall them for Barney when the time came.

The dispatcher answered the phone and I relayed the particulars of the situation. My familiarity with Belle Harbor was growing, but much of the place was still new to me. To the best of my ability I described the location at the base of the lighthouse, near the rocks, at the bottom of the cliff, and near the trail. Thankfully, the woman on the other end of the line knew the place intimately and alerted the deputy to head our way. She checked the tide tables while we were on the phone to calculate how much time we had before the water surrounded us. Her estimation was about an hour. I glanced back at the waves and hoped it was that long. She assured me the deputy was en route and we disconnected.

Fiona paced, kicking the sand. I returned to her side. "If you need to get back to work, I'm fine waiting here. It shouldn't be long now."

She extended her arm toward me and tilted her head with a melancholy smile. "Are you sure?" She squinted toward Poppy. "I don't even know if I can focus. But I should check in with my crew and see if they need anything." She grabbed me in a tight bear hug, then extended her arms and peered into my eyes. "Thank you." She sniffed and retraced our steps to climb back over the rocks.

When the tide was all the way out, you could walk past the rocks without hiking over them to gain access to the location. But for now, that was the only way out, except for the steep trail up the cliff.

I moved back to the location I had called from and sat on a rock in the corner. The sun beat down on the sand and Poppy's body. The wild waves glistened with the ebb and flow, the sound obscuring my beating heart. I looked around for any other people, not sure what I would say if anyone happened upon us. In the distance, the siren of the police car alerted me to the impending arrival of law enforcement. By now, Uncle Jack probably wondered where I was. My short jaunt for a quick ride on the Ferris wheel had extended significantly longer than a break from my baking.

The siren ceased. The deputy appeared at the top of the cliff, shaded his eyes, and inspected the area. He gave a slight wave, then looked around, pondering how to descend the cliff. The easiest way was most likely sliding down on his bottom. Instead, he chose to slowly step along the root paths to support his descent. The last ten feet of the trail, he jogged over to join me.

As I watched him navigate the arduous route, I noticed about a third of the way up from the sand, the path split off in another direction that veered toward the lighthouse. That must be where I saw the jogger escape from my vantage point at the top of the Ferris wheel. My eyes followed where I expected that path to lead, past the lighthouse and out to the road. Shrubs grew wild on both sides, almost hiding it from view. I looked up again. Did the jogger push Poppy over the cliff and disappear down that path? Who was he and why would he do that?

I shivered as the deputy approached me with his notebook out. He looked at his watch. We didn't have much time. I closed my eyes again, visualizing details as I shared them with the deputy. Poor Poppy.

CHAPTER THREE

The overhead lights at Checkered Past Antiques shone down on the endless treasures that Uncle Jack had gathered over the years. He had recently installed spotlights like you would see in an art gallery to emphasize some of the more collectible pieces. Since I had arrived in Belle Harbor, the layout of the place had drastically changed. For the better, in my opinion. I stopped and gazed around. There was significantly more order. More than just piles of stuff on tables, Uncle Jack had acquired glass display cases, shelving, and a few smaller tables to showcase different items each week. The volume of customers had more than doubled.

"Unkie, here's another piece of the tea set," I said.

He took the cup and faked drinking from it with his pinkie finger stuck out. The pattern of the cup was almost identical to the decor that our business neighbor Florence had in her bookstore. We periodically discovered another piece of the set each time we dug through the antiques, finally accumulating eight cups and eight dessert plates. Uncle Jack placed the cup in the front display window.

"What do you think about giving that set to Florence? I think it would be a nice gesture and get us some goodwill with her?" I asked. I dusted off an old-time radio and gathered it next to other electronic items on a corner shelf. The word electronic was generous. I doubted much of this stuff would work anymore without an overhaul. But they were adorable pieces. The rotary phone, which rang every now and then, had been quiet for quite some time.

"That's a great idea. Her book club will love it," Unkie said.

"I'm happy to pay for it." I retrieved an empty cardboard box from under a table. We hadn't gotten off to a great start with Florence when she moved in. In fact, she almost didn't—finding a dead body in your new store would put a lot of people off. I carefully wrapped and packed the tea set for delivery. My hand slipped and a plate clinked against a cup. I lifted them both, inspecting for damage. My brain was elsewhere.

"Til?" Uncle Jack crouched next to me and the box, bones creaking as he assisted my packing.

I looked up, my face slack. I couldn't hide anything from him. I shrugged and inhaled deeply. "Why would someone want to hurt Poppy?" I asked.

He took the plate and wrapping paper from my hand and finished folding, gently stacking the piece in the box. "From everything I know, she was a nice lady."

I sat back on my heels.

"Her husband must be devastated," Uncle Jack said. "I don't know if he'll want to keep the restaurant. Poppy's Pizza Parlor was all hers."

"I didn't know she was married." I stood, allowing the circulation to return to my legs.

Pushing himself up with his hands, Uncle Jack said, "Sadly, the spouse is always a suspect when something happens. I just hope Barney expedites his investigation."

We had been working our tails off to straighten and clean the antique shop in anticipation of a visit by the president of the business owner's association. The annual Arts Walk was in a few days. It was a weekend-long street party, with live music, theatrical performances, and the conversion of the boardwalk into one big gallery. It showcased the best of local arts and culture, a highlight of Belle Harbor's cultural calendar. Fiona had been crazy busy preparing her menu of nibbles and drinks for one of the biggest moneymakers of the year.

Right on cue, Hazel North swooped into the shop, clipboard in hand as if she were grading us. Which she probably was. She stood just inside the door, slowly turning her head one hundred and eighty degrees from left to right. "Well, it looks better. But..." She took a couple more steps and touched a tabletop, raising her finger. "Still more dusting to do."

"Nice to see you, Hazel," Uncle Jack said in his cheeriest voice, attempting to make nice to the woman who could cause a lot of drama.

"Look. I know you have a lot of... stuff in here." Hazel emphasized the word *stuff* and paused, appearing to contemplate her next words. "But if we're going to be able to attract visitors from all over to the Arts Walk, you're going to have to spruce up some more." She bowed her head and tapped her pen on the clipboard. She lifted a sheet of paper and began making notes.

Unkie looked at me and shrugged. I was sure we both wondered what infraction she was writing us up for this time. Hazel was not above petty fines. And if you didn't pay, the local newspaper that she owned would make it well known that you were a scofflaw for skipping out on a few bucks. Uncle Jack always paid his fines whether he agreed with them or not. And never one to miss an opportunity to spread sunshine with his bubbly personality, he attached positive notes to the payment. I suspected if Hazel did see them, they hadn't made much of an impression to date.

"We're on it, Hazel," Uncle Jack said in his peppiest voice.

"We've got a lot of bad publicity to overcome. With that Poppy dying, after all." Hazel flipped a few more pages on her clipboard and wrote several more notes. "Although"—she lifted her head—"that woman's place was messier than this." Hazel swept her arm around the room. "I can't tell you how many times I wrote her up. Sand on the front stoop all the time. Napkins flying away from the outdoor seating. A disaster." She shook her head.

"Hello." We all swiveled our heads to the front, grateful for the interruption. Barney stepped inside and removed his hat. "Nice to see you again, Hazel." He moved toward her, his arm outstretched to shake her hand.

She turned away and tucked the clipboard under her arm, hiking her purse strap onto her shoulder. "I'll be back before Arts Walk to re-inspect," Hazel said and escaped through the front door.

Barney smirked. His strategy for sweetness, similar to Uncle Jack's, apparently had no effect on Hazel. "I can't see how those two are sisters. Florence is nothing like her," Barney said.

Uncle Jack's eyes widened and he pursed his lips, staring at me.

Barney pointed at him. "Not a word, mister. If you got to know Florence, you'd see what I mean." Barney and Florence had hit it off, eventually. Once she found out he was a bookworm and wanted to join a book club, the two of them had been inseparable.

Uncle Jack held up his hands. "Anything you do that irritates Hazel is OK in my book," Uncle Jack said.

"Unkie!" I fist bumped his shoulder.

"Well, eventually I'm going to crack her crusty exterior. Mark my words," Uncle Jack said.

I had no doubt.

"Any word on Poppy?" I asked.

Barney angled his head toward me. "Not yet, hon. I think your instincts are spot on, though." He looked at Uncle Jack. "There were scuff marks at the top of the cliff like someone struggled. It doesn't look like she jumped or fell."

I shuddered, lifting the box we packed for Florence and placing it in a corner. I hoped our gift would endear us just a bit more to our business neighbor. And if Uncle Jack minded his snarky manners, this just might work.

CHAPTER FOUR

I was bound and determined to find a way to improve our relationship with Florence. Today I was experimenting with something completely out of the ordinary. But nothing ventured, nothing gained. If I could pull off this baking feat, I was convinced it would get Florence on our good side for quite some time. Florence had created a cozy location in the corner of the store for her monthly book club meetings. It was decked out with a round table covered in a floral tablecloth, just ripe for tea and crumpets. Typically my baking items didn't call for yeast, so I was nervous about making sure I followed the recipe to a T. I slowly stirred the sugar and yeast into the warm milk. Small bubbles formed around the perimeter of the bowl. That seemed like a good sign. I set the timer for ten minutes and wandered through the shop.

I really hoped we passed inspection on Hazel's second visit. I gandered at the displays, lighted for maximum emphasis. In my humble opinion, the place looked outstanding. I wandered through the aisles with the eye of a customer. If there were something specific I was looking for, would it be easy-peasy to find it? And if there wasn't? It would be an adventure discovering the incredibly eclectic mix of wares. Uncle Jack regularly worked with estate sales in acquiring new pieces. It was clear why he enjoyed the work. Being the people person he was, he was always up for a good story. And these antiques were full of lore. The timer dinged and I returned to the kitchen.

I pulled the mixer to the center of the counter and loaded the ingredients into the bowl. I attached the paddle, turned the knob to low, and began the kneading. Peering inside, I saw that the dough formed and wobbled around. So far, so good. Next step, let it rise for a couple of hours. I covered the bowl loosely with plastic and set it aside. I looked at my watch. Unkie was normally here by now. Every time he was late, my brain went from zero to calamity in one second. Uncle Jack was in good health, but still, he was in his seventies. I really hoped he was OK. I dusted the flour off the mixer, thinking about the errand I needed to run. Unkie wouldn't hesitate to leave the shop unattended, but I wasn't convinced that was a good business practice.

I moved to the checkout counter and rummaged for a piece of paper and pen. I'd at least leave a note detailing my plans. With my back to the door, I hadn't seen Uncle Jack enter the store.

"Oh no. Not again," he said.

I whipped my head around. "You have got to quit startling me like that!" I put my hand over my heart and handed him the note I had written. "And not again what?"

Unkie held his nose. "Smells like Willie might have nabbed another mouse and stashed it for me to find." He read the note. "To the wharf again?" His grin spanned from ear to ear. Planning his birthday had been one of my greatest joys since returning to Belle Harbor.

"Yes. And the smell is yeast. I'm trying that crumpet recipe for Florence. But they need to rise for a couple of hours." I looked around. "You OK here without me?"

He tipped his head. "Go. I'll be fine."

"Love you, Unkie." I sped to the back of the shop, removed my apron, and grabbed my backpack. The day was still early enough that I would enjoy a cool walk.

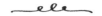

The sun angle was just above the houses on the hill to my left as I headed south to the cruise rental shop. In about an hour it would be fully showering the beach in glorious warmth. I followed the path from the sidewalk next to the shops out to the boardwalk that ran the length of the beach. I hooked my thumbs through the straps at my shoulders and lengthened my stride. Not many people were at the beach, but that would soon change.

I had gotten to a good pace as I neared the end of the boardwalk that intersected the many shops at the wharf. I turned left, away from the ocean, to navigate to my destination. The lady running the new cotton candy stand was just setting up and raised her hand in a wave. Behind her, in a row of shops bordering the parking lot was a large sign indicating Poppy's Pizza Parlor. From the outside, it looked perfectly fine, unlike Hazel's description of a dump. I hoped for the family's sake that they could continue the business, if that's what they wanted.

I pushed open the door to the cooler air of the cruise rental. Ruthie greeted me and accepted my final payment. "Would you like a quick tour?" she asked.

"OK." I hadn't planned on it, but why not? I followed her through the back door out to the mooring. She led me to the most unusual thing I'd ever seen. The pictures did not do it justice.

Ruthie extended her arm toward the bus. "You can board it if you want." She removed the rope blocking the entrance.

I looked at her. "I'm kind of in a hurry, but this is even better than I hoped for." The inside of the floating vintage Thomas International school bus was decked out like a living room. Wooden floors, a light mint green ceiling, booths with cushions along the sides. This really would be an epic party for my amazing uncle.

"That's usually the reaction we get." She replaced the rope. "We look forward to seeing you soon."

I turned and started toward the parking lot. "Thank you so much." The sun was now higher, the temperature warming up. I headed to the sidewalk that bordered the shops to get some shade as I returned to the antique shop. Just enough time would have passed for the dough to rise for the crumpets by the time I got back. A line had formed at the cotton candy stand, the lady handing out the brightly colored fluffs on a stick.

Just to the other side of the line, a guy ran by, wearing the same outfit as the person I saw the other day running from the scene with Poppy. He moved quickly, but the blur looked identical with a baseball cap, beard, and glasses. Who was this guy? And did he have something to do with Poppy's death? I sped around the cotton candy line to follow him, but my jog wasn't fast enough to keep up. He darted between buildings out to the main street behind the shops that lined the beach. I cut through to follow him. By the time I got to the street the distance between us had doubled.

I picked up my pace as much as I could, my backpack bobbing up and down, my breath gasping. No way I would catch him. But maybe I could keep him in my sights to see where he ended up. He crossed the street to the sidewalk along the front of the cottages, one of which was mine. He slowed just a bit as two of my neighbors' chickens darted out to the road. For the life of me, I don't know how those hens got out of the fence, but they seemed to be everywhere.

He crossed back toward the beach and disappeared. I was done. My side felt like I had been punched. I stopped and bent over, wheezing. I lifted my head, hoping the guy would pop back out from between the buildings. No luck. I had lost him. My gut said there was a connection between him and Poppy, and I needed to find out what it was.

CHAPTER FIVE

With my head up and shoulders back I pulled the little wagon along the sidewalk from the antique shop to Mocha Joe's Coffee Shop. My confidence soared with the business deal I had with Joe to provide him cupcakes and muffins every Tuesday and Thursday. I had perfected my routine to make the supply he had ordered. And by all accounts from Joe, the pastries disappeared as soon as they arrived.

Making a few dozen muffins and cupcakes every week was one thing, but more than that became serious business. I hoped to increase my production, but at the same time, feelings of impostor syndrome consumed me. Who was I, a forty-something divorced woman from Boston, to have a thriving bakery? Why did I ever think I could do this?

I shook my head, flinging those negatives thoughts away and returning to my rightly earned confidence. *One step at a time, Tilly.*

Signs in the window of Mocha Joe's advertised the upcoming Arts Walk. A local sculptor was booked to show her art at the coffee shop. I hoped to break away from the antique shop during the event to tour the different venues and take in the work of the artists.

I slowed my wagon and parked it next to the wall in front of the coffee shop. I hoisted the boxes and entered the always-packed lobby. The line of customers extended from the counter to the door. The smell of fresh coffee enveloped me, always a comforting aroma. I waited at the end of the line for a minute to assess my options. I didn't want people to think I was cutting in front of them, even though I wasn't ordering. I had some time on my hands for the moment, so I patiently waited my turn.

I turned and gazed out the front window toward the ocean, the waves gently ebbing and flowing, caressing the sand. My mind drifted to the sight of Poppy laying on the beach at the bottom of the cliff. What happened now? Would her pizza place go out of business? Had she arranged for an artist to display their work there? Fiona and I needed a field trip for dinner. She had been working her tail off in preparation for the Arts Walk, but my new friend had become my unofficial sleuthing partner. Maybe a visit to Poppy's would enlighten us about events prior to her untimely demise.

The line steadily moved forward, the well-oiled machine of baristas serving customers. I decided to wait my turn and take the opportunity to catch my breath. Uncle Jack and I had been uber busy at the antique shop and it was nice to have a change of pace.

Voices from the corner of the shop caught my ear above the din of pounding out used coffee grounds from the espresso machine. Joe's arms waved in an expression of frustration, his brows furrowed, his head tilted. A woman pointed her finger in Joe's face as if scolding him. Her short auburn hair bobbed as she talked. The man to her side stood shoulders slumped. I could see even hidden by his facial hair that his lips were pursed, probably hoped she would stop her outburst. Joe shook his head and threw up his arms, stomping away from the duo.

The couple took a seat at a two-person table near the window. The man gripped his cup, staring away from the woman. I looked toward the other side of the cafe, not wanting to feel like I was intruding into a private matter, albeit one that happened in a public place. I kept my back to them but continued to hear their animated discussion.

"Stella, why do you treat people that way?" the man asked. "Joe has done nothing but pay his rent on time. And his business brings a lot of people to the boardwalk."

"Troy, you know nothing about business. If they're doing well, it's only right they pay more to help the town," Stella said.

The line steadily moved toward the front counter and I returned to facing front. I now stood only a few feet from the couple, seeing their heads bowed toward each other.

"Besides, if you weren't so busy with your hussy on the side, you'd know that." The woman huffed, sitting back in her chair. She sipped the coffee, loudly clinking the ceramic cup back on the saucer.

"Stella," the man started.

She held up her hand. "Don't even. We just need to put this all behind us."

I was two places from the front of the line. Joe had his game face on and hadn't spotted me. I was sure if he had, he'd wave me to the front. The older gentleman in front of me placed his order for coffee, the old-fashioned kind, he said. I assumed he wanted a drip, nothing with froth, syrups, or cream. "And one of those cupcakes," he added.

The barista looked into the display case and returned to the counter. "I'm sorry sir. We're all out of those. They're very popular."

I stepped forward. "Looks like I'm just in time," I said. The man wheeled around, his mouth in a frown. His expression looked like he was prepared to admonish someone cutting the line and rudely interrupting.

He looked down at the boxes I held. "You don't mean...?" he asked.

"Tilly." Joe skirted the end of the counter and claimed the boxes from my arms. His eyes widened and he mouthed *thank you*.

"Well, little lady. You're the one I have to thank for my growing waistline?" The elderly man grinned and patted his belly.

I chuckled. "I guess so."

I moved to the end of the counter for a quick chat with Joe.

He handed the box to one of his employees to unpack the items. "That's a common occurrence," he said.

I still couldn't fathom that I got to do something I really enjoyed—and people paid me for it. I gulped. Maybe it was time to take this up a notch. *Jump in before you're ready.* I heard Uncle Jack's encouraging words in my head. "Joe..." I began.

He looked up from his work. Maybe now wasn't the time. He was busy loading cups and lids into the storage unit for the barista to easily retrieve them for each order. And just as quickly he began replenishing napkins into dispensers.

What was the worst he could say? No. And then I would move on.

"Tilly, I could really use about double the order you've been providing. Could you do that?" he blurted out, as if reading my mind. His movements smoothly shifted from one task to another, keeping his team fully supplied with what they needed to serve customers.

I grabbed the counter, my head slightly spinning. Double the order meant I would need to rearrange my routine to produce that much. Not a problem. Thoughts raced through my brain for how I might organize to accomplish the request. I made mental notes about additional supplies I would need, but my biggest question was about time to fulfill the request. By myself, a couple dozen twice a week was doable. More than that meant I would likely need some kind of assistance.

"Tilly?" Joe said.

"Oh, um, yeah. You got it. I'll have that starting Thursday," I said.

"Thanks. Look, I gotta run. Some time we should get together when we can chat longer without my always getting interrupted with work." He turned and grabbed two full cups from the counter and called out the names of customers to retrieve them.

My smile quickly disappeared. I agreed to an order without much of a plan. *Oh, Uncle Jack. I hope you'll agree to help me until I can get my act together.* I didn't have a clue how to go about finding a permanent assistant. I followed a customer from the store and mindlessly grabbed the handle of my wagon, returning to the antique shop.

CHAPTER SIX

Four in the morning was earlier than even Mocha Joe's was open. I had brewed a pot of coffee, already finished it, and had a second one in progress. I decided the night before to get in to the antique shop and set up before Unkie arrived. My strategy was to lay everything out in assembly-line fashion and Uncle Jack would just have to follow instructions. I couldn't afford his "help" like the first time around with the cupcakes. One wrong move with customers and it would take a gargantuan effort to overcome bad publicity. His heart was in the right place, just not his baking skills.

My counter teemed with measuring cups and spoons, the ingredients all in order of need, baking tins, and paper cupcake liners. I stood back and scanned the system. This is what a professional baker's kitchen looked like. I scooted thoughts from my brain about moving my operation to another location. I knew at some point I would outgrow the kitchen Unkie had built for me inside of his antique shop. There was no more loving of a gesture than carving out his own space for his niece. With the growing number of orders and need for an assistant, it wouldn't be long before I outgrew the place.

My tummy swirled with the thoughts of changing a good thing. I wanted the feeling of joy I had when I was inside this place to continue forever. Maybe Uncle Jack and I could move together to a larger place. Would that work? He would probably do anything for me. But that would mean leaving the location he and Uncle Frank had been at for so long. Nah. At some point, I had to be on my own. I shook my head. For today, I would enjoy this experience with my uncle.

The front door squeaked quietly as Unkie arrived. The bags under his eyes begged for coffee to perk him up. "This is early, even for me." I escorted him to the back of the store and poured him a steaming cup. He looked toward the kitchen. "You've been here a while."

"I just got a few things organized," I said.

He gulped down half of the coffee. "You just order me around. Whatever you need." He looked at me, his lips pursed and the corners of his mouth raised.

"Thank you." I led him to the kitchen and swept my arm around. "So here's how this is going to go." I stepped to the counter and pointed. "I measure ingredients, you put them into the mixer and mix." I stepped around him and continued, "Then you line the baking tins. I take the batter and pour into the tins." I put my hands on my hips and faced him. "Sound good?"

He giggled.

"What?" I asked. I retrieved aprons from the hook on the wall and handed him one.

"You are large and in charge. That's all." He turned his back toward me to tie his apron string behind him.

"And you look adorable in that apron with the dish running away with the spoon," I said.

He stepped to his station ready to begin, his arms in the air. "I feel like there should be a starter's pistol to begin the race."

I filled cups and spoons with ingredients and placed them in the mixing bowl. "Focus, Unkie," I said.

He turned, saluted me, and started the mixer on low. And we were off. Silently we continued our process for four batches of the muffins. Uncle Jack turned off the mixer and looked at me. "If you'd told me a year ago I'd be in a kitchen in the corner of my antique shop making muffins, I would have said you're out of your mind." He reached his arms around me as I carefully filled the muffin tins. "But there's nowhere else on the planet I would want to be. Thank you for bringing me more joy in my life."

"Are you kidding me?" I asked. Using the measuring cup, I scraped the remainder of the batter into the last open tin and placed the pan in the oven. "Unkie, *you* rescued *me*." I stood back and looked at him, covering my mouth with my arm. He had managed to cover himself head to toe in flour.

He looked down and stretched his apron out to examine it. "How did that happen? I was so careful this time." He lifted his head with a serious expression.

I reached up and ruffled his thinning hair. "And somehow you've managed to get it all the way up here." I removed my apron and hung it on the hook. "Why don't we take a break before we start the cupcakes? I'll clean up, then get them ready."

"That settles it. You need to get an official assistant. I'm nervous that I'm going to mess something up," he said.

"I'll think about it," I said. We settled in for another cup of coffee and a warm muffin. "Have you heard anything from Barney about Poppy?" I bit into the treat and followed it with a swallow of coffee.

"You know how he is. Saying something without saying anything at all," he said.

SUE HOLLOWELL

"The thing is…" What was I doing? There was no reason to believe the guy I saw was involved with Poppy's murder. There had to be a logical explanation why he had been running from the scene. I hoped. Oh dear, I hoped hard. "I saw someone near Poppy's body. I told the officer, but it's really bothering me."

"That's all you can do," Uncle Jack said and gobbled the remainder of the muffin.

I couldn't keep secrets from him. "I followed the guy a couple of days ago." I lifted my head. "He was running near the wharf." I put my cup on the table, picking up Willie, who had quietly appeared from under the table.

"Tilly," he admonished as he rose and petted the cat.

Willie sat on my lap and closed his eyes, soaking up the attention. I gazed out the front windows of the antique shop, the daylight dawning. I knew he was right, but it was hard to mind my own business when my gut was sending different messages. I just couldn't decipher the meaning yet. I stood and put Willie on the chair, where he circled up in the warmth left by my seat.

The door squeaked again, rescuing me. "Hey Jack," Justin said. "I'm glad you're here."

Unkie looked at me and shrugged.

"I mean. Oh, I don't know. I'm so flustered," Justin said, looking down at his hands. Willie leapt from the chair and rubbed against Justin's bare leg. He wore his standard outfit of T-shirt, shorts, and flip-flops. "I wanted to tell you, I'm not sure how I'm going to pay my rent."

Uncle Jack placed a hand on Justin's shoulder. "What's going on?"

Justin plopped into a chair, followed by Willie jumping on his lap. "Hazel," he uttered.

Uncle Jack's eyes got big and he looked back and forth between Justin and me.

"She's written me up again at the store. I think I'm going to get evicted." Justin leaned his elbow on the table, his head in his hand. "It's ridiculous, of course. But that doesn't matter."

Even though the state had legalized marijuana, controversy swirled around the businesses who sold it. Justin was feeling Hazel's wrath.

"She said the riffraff coming into my business are bringing down property values and scaring customers away from nearby shops." Justin sighed. "This might just be the final straw that sends me packing back to the Midwest."

Uncle Jack stepped forward. "Not if I have anything to say about it. Hang in there. This ain't over."

My uncle was never one to let someone be wronged. I was confident Justin had the staunchest advocate on his side. There might just be a showdown at the business owners' association meeting tomorrow night. I only hoped Uncle Jack didn't pay the price by losing his own shop.

I stepped forward. "Uncle Jack, do you really think you can help Justin?" My face flushed. My brain was apparently not in alignment with the rest of my body. I had ignored my feelings for Justin because I wasn't even sure what they meant. He was easy on the eyes and very kind. I needed some time to sort this out. But if he was gone, that would make my decision for me, and I wasn't ready to have my hand forced. I wanted to see where our relationship naturally led.

CHAPTER SEVEN

The room had tables laid out in a square. One side had microphones placed at several spots. A small crowd in the corner on the left whispered, somber faces as if we were attending a funeral. I pointed to two chairs on the right side of the tables, and Uncle Jack and I took our seats. Attending the meeting of the business owners' association wasn't my idea of where to spend my time, but Uncle Jack convinced me that it would be worth my while. A pile of papers sat in random locations around the tables. I slid one from the top of the pile and saw a map of the locations where artists would display their work at the different businesses in town during Arts Walk. Three locations had big *X*'s through them, one of which was Poppy's Pizza Parlor. I elbowed Uncle Jack and handed him the paper.

His bushy brows furrowed. He leaned over and pointed to the largest *X*. Justin's marijuana store. He had complained to Unkie that Hazel had it in for him. Some people retained old ideas about drug dealers and the people that conducted business there. Hazel topped that list. Though some of Justin's customers were the nicest people—and upstanding citizens in the community—if Hazel wanted him gone, he was done for.

The room began to fill with other business owners as the time neared the top of the hour. The owner of Daffy Taffy, the candy store, waved to Uncle Jack.

The small group in the front corner broke up and took their seats at the head of the table, Hazel sitting front and center. Stella, with her bright fuchsia lipstick, was to her right. Stella's husband moved along the tables to a space opposite those two. Who could blame him? I wouldn't want to be associated with them either.

Hazel gaveled the group to order and our little town business owners' association meeting was underway. I placed my notebook and pen on the table and scooted my chair in, ready for taking notes.

"First order of the day," Hazel began. "Several businesses have earned citations in the last week." She pulled a sheet of paper toward her and tipped her head. She read the names of the four who had been fined.

"May I speak?" The owner of Daffy Taffy stood.

Hazel lifted her head, still peering over the top of her glasses, acknowledging the man but not directly permitting his speaking.

"I'd like to appeal my fine." He looked around for moral support, appearing to assess whether to continue. He cleared his throat. "Finding one wrapper on the beach from my store shouldn't get me a fine. That's out of my control."

Hazel continued her glare.

The man sat.

"Your wrapper, your responsibility." Hazel slammed the gavel so hard that it shook the table, sloshing water from a glass.

Stella looked at Hazel, and her bright neon lips grinned. I envisioned Stella's lips on Hazel's behind. What a suck-up. Stella grabbed a napkin and dabbed up the escaping liquid.

"Anyone else?" Hazel swept the gavel from right to left, jabbing the air. "I didn't think so." She gently laid it on the pad, patting it. "Next on our agenda is the report from the planning committee about expansion. Stella?"

"Thank you, Madam President." Stella nodded toward Hazel.

Unkie leaned over and whispered, "Can you hear that kissing noise?"

I whipped my head toward him. He had read my mind. I placed my pointer finger over my lips. That's all we needed, Uncle Jack banned from the meetings, and possibly worse. How he had survived without snarky comments all this time, I couldn't fathom.

"First, as you can see by the revised maps on the tables, we've had to exclude some businesses from the Arts Walk. I'm sure you understand why." If Stella's tone was any sweeter, syrup would be dripping from her mouth. "Second." Stella took the pile of papers, brought one forward, and held it up. "Here it is. I'm pleased to say that the property at the end of the pier has been purchased by the town and will now be leased to several high-end shops. The first to agree to come is COACH." Stella leaned over and hefted her large bag for all to see.

"That's just wonderful, Stella," Hazel interjected. "Our vision for upscale shops is finally materializing. And it will do wonders for the town budget."

Uncle Jack stood. I closed my eyes. Was this the beginning of the end? What did he have up his sleeve? I swallowed, wishing myself to be transported anywhere but here.

"Madam President," he began. This had a chance to end well after all. "If I may."

Hazel nodded.

Regardless of his thoughts toward Hazel and her position, Unkie knew politics and how to play the game when he wanted to. "With all due respect, I think we should carefully consider before approving chain stores to take up in our town."

Hazel stared. Was Uncle Jack going down? In the silence, people fidgeted in their chairs.

"All that I wanted to say is that the charm of our unique shops gives this a small-town feel. Most people come for that atmosphere, and I wouldn't want anything to deter from that." Unkie plunked down in his chair, saying his piece.

I reached over and placed my hand on his arm.

"Noted. We'll take that under advisement," Hazel said.

I doubted his suggestion would get any airtime at their next meeting. Hazel and Stella appeared determined to get shops that most people in the town probably couldn't afford.

"Finally, I'd like to share that the town budget has just enough money that we can do some additional beautification for the Arts Walk. The mayor informed me we can budget a thousand dollars," Hazel said.

Stella sat tall in her chair. "And that will go to a pot of flowers for each of you, courtesy of Troy's store."

The entire room looked at Troy, who sat at a table in the corner, as far as he could get from Stella. His face reddened and he slightly raised his hand, acknowledging the attention.

The gavel slammed and we all jumped as Hazel said, "Meeting adjourned."

Uncle Jack and I stood. I mumbled, "If I never come to another business owners' association meeting, it will be too soon."

"Ah, Til. You just need to learn the rules. Then you can play the game to your advantage," Uncle Jack said.

I touched his elbow, guiding us out of the room. Before we had escaped, I heard "Jack, wait up."

I turned and saw Stella quickly approaching. So close to being out of here. "I wanted to give you a card in case you wanted to get more flowers than the one pot provided by the town." Stella removed her large designer bag from her shoulder and buried her hand inside. "Where is that?" She pulled out a few things and dropped them back inside. She looked up and grinned. "I can't find anything in here ever since my bag got tipped upside down." Finally extracting her arm she said, "Aha," and handed Uncle Jack a business card. "Just give Troy a call. He'll get you a deal."

"Thanks, Stella," Uncle Jack said to her backside as she had already moved on to deal out cards to the remaining business owners in the room. We entered the lobby and Unkie promptly deposited the card in the trash.

I giggled as we sped through the automatic doors to the fresh air outside.

CHAPTER EIGHT

I sat on the step of my front porch, lacing up my new running shoes. I didn't know if this was a hairbrained idea or not. I was an active kid but definitely not the athlete in the family like my brother. It would do me good to get in better shape. I had decided to run to the lighthouse, then to the antique shop. I had no sense of distance, so I didn't know if it was half a mile or five miles. I stood and stretched because that's what I saw other runners do before they started.

The sun was rising from behind the cottages, highlighting blue sky and coloring the ocean a bright teal. I began my snail's pace. I could probably walk faster than I was running. But it was a start. Rarely was the temperature too cool to not be outside in short sleeves. An elderly couple on their porch raised their coffee cups to me as I passed by. I waved and smiled. My brain thought that if anything happened to me they would be witnesses to my location at this early hour.

My feet pounded the pavement, establishing a rhythm. I wasn't sure how my arms were to behave, so I slowly swung them in short strokes from front to back. I wondered if that awkward feeling would pass. I had passed about five cottages and my calves reminded me of my attempted jog the other day. I stopped for a second and tilted my toes back toward my shin for a stretch. Sorry, legs. I decided to walk the distance of the next block, then pick up the jog again. Maybe intervals would be the best bet for now until I could gain some endurance.

Another coffee drinker raised their cup to me. I hadn't expected an audience on my inaugural jaunt. I returned my gaze to the road ahead of me and spotted another jogger enter from between two buildings. I squinted and realized, sure enough, it was jogger man. He looked at me, turned right, and sped off. No way I could keep up with him. I just needed to keep him in my sights. His head swiveled back toward me again, and he increased his speed, crossing the road to the side nearest the ocean. Was he trying to escape? What was he trying to hide? I looked to my left to confirm there weren't any cars, and I crossed the road.

His lead was about six cottages in front of me—and gaining. He darted to the other side of the road again, as if trying to elude my follow. He would succeed. No way I could keep up. And what if I did catch him? I had no plan. I continued my walk-run alternation, now about halfway between my cottage and the lighthouse. If I could only keep him in sight until that point, I might be able to confirm my suspicion of his escape route—if he indeed was involved in Poppy's death. I stayed to my side of the road rather than waste a precious step to mimic his zig-zagging pattern.

A final time, he returned to my side of the road, almost to the base of the lighthouse. My side ached as if a knife penetrated my belly. I gasped to fill my lungs, the pain increasing. Shallow breaths weren't a good plan either. Passing out wouldn't get me anywhere. I slowed to a fast walk, furrowing my brows hard to focus my gaze on the jogger and watch his movement. He took a hard left for his final disappearance from my sight.

I stopped, my plan foiled to investigate this mysterious man and his involvement in Poppy's death. I inhaled deeply, the stabbing pain subsiding a bit. No need to jog any further. I walked and extended my stride to catch my breath. After another cottage length, I breathed in again, finally slowing my heart rate. I put my hand on my chest, realizing how fast my pulse raced, and continued a steady pace to the location where the man had disappeared. As I rounded the corner, I saw that the path jutted to the right. I stopped and stretched my neck toward the location above the cliff where Poppy had fallen. The path nowhere near intersected the location. Was it possible the guy was only on a run and had nothing to do with the murder? I had to get more evidence to avoid accusing someone of a heinous crime they had nothing to do with. Relief hit me. If he was innocent of any wrongdoing, maybe I could ditch the jogging and take up another activity more suited to me.

I turned in a full circle, looking at the entire location to envision how Poppy had fallen and the jogger played a part. I couldn't fix any logical scenario in my head. I started my trek to the antique shop, this time at a pace that didn't feel like it would kill me. I walked along the sidewalk next to the shops that bordered the beach and the boardwalk. A chunk of time must have passed since I started my journey earlier in the day. The sun now fully shone on the sand and the beach goers had set up shop for the day. The pace of my breath had normalized, but I looked down and saw I had sweated through the armpits of my shirt. I subtly sniffed it. Not too bad. Since I was on a break from baking, I could quickly head home to change.

"What have you been doing?" Uncle Jack greeted me as I entered Checkered Past Antiques.

"That's a good question," I answered as I headed back to the kitchen to prepare for baking.

"Tilly?" Uncle Jack persisted. He looked me up and down, waiting for an explanation.

I shuffled baking supplies around the counter, keeping my head down.

His shadow covered the counter. I looked up and smirked. "OK. I tried to follow that jogger again to the path near where Poppy fell. But don't worry. I'm pretty sure jogging is now off the table for me."

Unkie fidgeted with a set of measuring spoons. "Just don't get yourself into trouble."

My protector, my encourager, my friend.

We both lifted our heads at a sound that came from Justin's apartment upstairs. "Speaking of trouble," Uncle Jack said.

I followed him to the stairwell in the back of the shop. We ascended the creaky stairs. Halfway, Unkie turned to me and held out his arm to halt my progress. No way. I was joining him in our quest to discover the source of the noise. He flipped the switch, lighting the hallway, and continued his trek up the remaining steps. On the landing, he stretched his neck around the corner, then moved further along the path. He chuckled.

I joined him and saw a table on its side and an artificial flower basket upside down on the floor. Huddled next to the flower basket were two glowing eyes and a guilty face. I sighed, not realizing the tension I held in my diaphragm. I placed my hand on my stomach and breathed in again. "It's just Willie," I said.

Uncle Jack proceeded down the hallway toward the door to Justin's apartment, looking around. I scanned the sparse hallway to spot what he was searching for. "Is something wrong?" I asked.

He retraced his steps and picked Willie up. "Just looking for his partner in crime. The two of them are inseparable lately."

Ah, yes. Florence's cat, Gwinnie, and Willie had become fast friends. "I'm just glad it wasn't something worse. With Poppy's unsolved murder, I'm a little jumpy," I said. I righted the table and returned the flowers to their display location.

Uncle Jack gently placed his hand on my back, and the three of us returned to the antique shop.

CHAPTER NINE

I t was a rare treat that I got to have dinner with Fiona. Most nights she worked at her bar until the wee hours, way past my bedtime given that I had to rise early for baking duty. Though, with her new manager learning so quickly she felt comfortable leaving him in charge for an occasional girls night out. She deserved it. That woman worked her tail off and her business thrived because of her passion to serve her customers. Tonight we decided on pizza at Poppy's to support the family in their time of need. Sadly, the restaurant had only one other couple who were dining at the same time. I wondered if people stayed away because the stigma of the suspicious death of the owner.

We sat in a red, vinyl-lined booth along the wall. The background music attempted to brighten the spirits of the empty place. As Fiona leaned in, the vinyl squeaked loudly. She said, "How's the baking going?"

I looked around and almost felt like I needed to whisper. I matched her posture and said, "Great. Joe doubled his order. Uncle Jack is helping me with production. But even he agrees I'm ready to hire an official baking assistant."

"That's great," Fiona said. "I'll let you know if I think of anyone that would be a good fit."

The server crossed the room from the only other occupied table and approached to take our order. "Hi ladies, what can I get you?"

Fiona looked at me and said, "Do you want to start with a glass of wine?"

I nodded.

"OK, how about the house red? Why don't we order a couple of pizza, then we can take leftovers?" Fiona said.

I pulled the menu toward me. "I haven't really had a chance to decide. Could you give us a minute?" I asked the server.

"Of course. I'll get your drinks," he said and headed toward the kitchen.

"Why don't we each choose one, then we can share?" I suggested. The choices were plenty and every single one sounded like a must have. "How is the classic pepperoni?"

Fiona wrinkled her nose. "Normally I wouldn't dis another person's business. But last time I was here, that wasn't good. I heard the owner had subbed in turkey instead of beef. Putrid." She gave a thumbs-down gesture.

We continued studying the menu and settled on our choices. The server brought our wine and we placed our orders.

I lifted my glass and held it toward Fiona. "Cheers," I said. I swirled the red liquid, taking a sip. "I'm trying a new recipe to see if I can make nice with Florence. Somehow I think she still blames us for the dead body in the bookstore before she opened for business."

Fiona's eyebrows raised. "Oh? This sounds interesting."

"I think it will either be a huge success or a fabulous disaster," I said.

She laughed. I relaxed. Being with her was so easy. "Unkie and I thought it would fit her theme at the bookstore. Remember that tea set we found at the antique shop?"

Fiona nodded as she sipped her wine.

"Along with giving her that, I've decided to make some traditional crumpets. My first batch actually came out pretty good," I said.

"That sounds far from your normal," Fiona said.

The server appeared from behind the swinging door to the kitchen and approached. "It should be just a couple of minutes now. Can I get you a refill?"

I looked at Fiona, who shrugged. "Sure," I answered. The server retraced his route. As the door swung open, I gasped and covered my mouth. My eyes popped wide open.

Fiona turned to see what I was looking at. "What is it?" She looked back at me.

The door had closed, obscuring both of our views of the kitchen. Maybe that split-second glimpse was playing with my brain. Or maybe it was the wine. I couldn't believe what I just saw.

"Tilly, you're scaring me. What's going on?" Fiona scooted to the edge of the booth and craned her neck toward the kitchen, still unable to see what I spotted from my vantage point.

"I think I'm just tired and my eyes are playing tricks on me," I said.

Fiona shook her head. "I'm not buying it. Something else is going on. Spill it."

"OK." I took another sip of liquid courage. "The guy I saw in the kitchen looked just like the one I saw running from Poppy's body the other day when I found her."

Fiona stood on her tiptoes to get a look through the door. She took two steps closer.

"Fiona," I whispered. The other couple looked our direction at the small disruption.

She waved her arm at me to simmer down. She continued behind the counter and peeked her head through the door. That woman seemed to have no fear. My stomach was in knots just from her simple spying.

She returned to the table. "That's Dean. He's the manager here. I wonder if you saw his twin brother Dave."

"They're twins?" I asked. I clasped my sweaty hands together in my lap.

"Yes. Identical."

I rubbed my hands on my shorts. "Well, that's a relief about Dean. But it doesn't remove Dave from my suspect list. I..." I clamped my mouth shut.

Fiona tilted her head. "What do you mean?"

I inhaled deeply and slowly breathed out. "OK." I looked at the couple across the way who were deep into devouring their delicious-looking pizza. "I might have spied on Dave."

"You what?!" Fiona exclaimed. She held her finger up at me. "And you didn't include me?"

"Well, when I first spotted Poppy from the Ferris wheel, I saw a guy running from the scene. I was afraid he had something to do with her death." I looked around to be sure we weren't being overheard. Maybe my theory was cockamamie, and I didn't want anyone else in on it, except Fiona.

"And?" Fiona prompted.

I gulped. Now was the time to loop in my friend. Maybe her perspective could help advance the clues. "I saw him again when I was at the wharf confirming Uncle Jack's party boat for his birthday."

"You're slow-walking me. What happened?" she continued.

"I tried to follow him. But he's an experienced runner. And let's just say I'm not. I wanted to find out who he was. So I went and bought running clothes and started running."

Fiona sat back in the booth. "This just keeps getting better. Don't keep me waiting." She giggled.

"Well, no clues yet. I was all geared up and tried to run, but I couldn't keep up with him. I followed him as far as the lighthouse. What I did find out is that I think he was on a totally different path from Poppy the other day when she fell." I couldn't be sure. But nobody else had entered the picture as a strong suspect. I had no idea how to confirm or deny his involvement that didn't include my passing out along the road.

"You need to be careful stalking people," she admonished.

I dipped my head. She was right. I didn't know this guy. And if I wasn't discreet, he might just turn on me. "I know."

"And next time, call me. I'll join you," she said. My partner in sleuthing.

CHAPTER TEN

The heat from the day had permeated the antique shop. Uncle Jack preferred the ocean breezes to naturally cool off the place rather than the air conditioner. I typically agreed with him. But today, the oven worked overtime getting the several batches of cupcakes prepared for the Arts Walk. My sweaty shirt stuck to my skin under the extra apron layer. *I may have to head home for a quick change of clothes before the festivities begin.* I made mini versions of my classic cream-filled cupcakes. I also created a tropical variety with almond cupcakes and coconut filling. I had already inhaled three of them. The small size made them too easy to indulge. There weren't many sweets that I didn't like, though. Today would provide a good indication if others liked them as well.

I plated up several of both cupcake flavors and headed to the display in the front window.

"Any extras for me?" Uncle Jack snagged a coconut mini off the tray. He closed his eyes and moaned. "Oh boy. I have to say, those might be even better than the other ones. Maybe I should try again to make sure." He reached toward the tray and I quickly moved away.

"I'll make you a batch later. These are for customers." I placed the cupcakes in the cooler. "I just hope people like them."

Uncle Jack continued to fiddle with several antiques, adjusting their positions. "Who cares if some don't like them? It just means you weren't meant for those people." He stepped to the other side of the table, moving more pieces. "Just concentrate on finding your people." He tilted his head, stood back, and eyed his handiwork. "I'm sure there are plenty of raving fans who will keep your business thriving."

I stepped to his side and hooked my arm through his, leaning my head on his shoulder. "It looks fabulous in here. Quit piddling around," I said. "I should get back to the kitchen. From what I hear, I may not have enough cupcakes."

"Especially if I keep sampling." Unkie chuckled at his own joke. "Well hello, Hazel." Uncle Jack's voice rose at least two octaves.

I turned and saw the president of the business owners' association with the clipboard in her arm. *I swear that thing is attached to her.*

"What do you think?" Uncle Jack swept his arm around the store. He was awfully bold asking her that. But then again, he generally had enough confidence not to care much what others thought. And he tried to share that with me.

Hazel took a few steps into the shop, looking at the cupcake display. She pointed with her pen. "What are those?" She gazed between Uncle Jack and me.

Unkie straightened his posture. "Just heaven in a cupcake. Would you like to try one?" He reached to open the case.

Hazel wrinkled her nose and shook her head. "Oh no." She ventured farther into the shop, looking left and right. She pivoted back toward the door. "Well, I guess this is as good as it's going to get. But maybe there won't be many visitors."

"I'll have you know, last year this shop was one of the top three locations visited during the Arts Walk," Uncle Jack said. He looked at me. All cordiality was gone from his demeanor. It took a lot for him to get upset, and Hazel certainly pushed his buttons. He shook his head.

Hazel scoffed. I always wondered about people who seemed to be mad at the world and what their home lives must have been like when they were a kid. What had happened in their world to turn their disposition so sour? "Well, now that we got rid of that Poppy's Pizza Parlor from the route, I'm hoping some of the other undesirables will follow." She stuck her nose in the air and swooped out the door like the wicked witch of the east.

I released my breath, not realizing I had been clenching my diaphragm. I approached Uncle Jack, prepared to salve any wounds left by that mean woman. "I hope you take your own advice. She's just not your people," I said.

He grinned. "Good one, Til. I do try to brush those remarks off quickly. But for some reason, that woman's comments get under my skin." He headed to the front corner of the store, preparing the area for the artist he had chosen to display her work at the antique shop. "I can't wait for you to meet Taylor." He had acquired a few easels and a table and chair as she had requested. "Her work is so fun. And so individual. Reminds me a bit of Mom." Unkie said "mom" in such a gentle tone. The legacy of Grandma Luna ran deep. And I was doing everything I could to live my best life and carry forward her baking traditions.

"Hello," a young gal said as she entered the shop.

Uncle Jack approached and retrieved the items that filled both of her hands. "Right on time. Taylor, meet my niece Tilly," Uncle Jack said.

"Nice to meet you," Taylor said. She must have been early twenties, a petite young woman with short brown, bobbed hair. Her jacket had been stitched with extra patches from different musical groups. Her black skinny jeans had ripped knees and topped bright green Converse high-tops.

"You too. I can't wait to see your work," I said. "I like your shoes." I held my leg out for her to see I also had Converse, though, in a bit more muted color.

"Cool," she said and followed Uncle Jack to the corner.

Together they unpacked her portfolio, placing the illustrations on the easels. "I actually have my own table and chair as part of the display, if you don't mind."

"Of course," Uncle Jack said. He grabbed both pieces and hauled them to the back of the store to make room for her things.

Taylor left to gather the remaining items.

Uncle Jack stood back, rubbing his chin, gazing at the display. "It's really different, isn't it?" he asked.

"It's great," I said. The illustrations were in the form of comics. One of them was of a T-shirt with pit stains titled *Busy Day*. I could totally relate to that.

Uncle Jack picked up a piece of paper that was the artist's biography and statement. He read from it, "Their interests lie in humor, honesty, and anxiety present in everyday life." He slipped it into a picture frame and hung it outside the shop for passersby to read.

Taylor returned with the furniture, painted white and trimmed with black lines. It fit perfectly to finish the display and make it look like a scene from a comic. It was brilliant. She pulled a book from her backpack and placed it on the table for the final piece. The black book with white letters was titled *Rejected Drawings*. She looked at us. "I can't thank you enough for taking a chance on me. Most people don't get my stuff."

"You are a perfect fit for this place. And we'd love it if you came every year," Uncle Jack said.

Cupcakes were one thing, but the creativity of Taylor was at another level. I was so impressed.

A head with a scruffy beard peeked through the door. "Just saying hi, guys," Barney said. "Heading next door to help Florence set up. Come by later." He waved and disappeared.

CHAPTER ELEVEN

T he crowds at the antique shop had come at a brisk pace. Of course, Taylor charmed them all with her engaging personality and sold several pieces. The cupcakes earned similar accolades and disappeared quickly. Fewer customers browsed the antiques, but Uncle Jack said he was OK with that. It was a night for the artists to shine, and Taylor's light was bright.

During a lull in the activity, Taylor took a seat with us at the coffee corner in the back of the store. "Thank you for letting me catch my breath. I'm exhausted." She wiped her brow, but she looked anything but beat. "And I am so grateful you allowed me to show my work in your store," she said.

"My dear, I wouldn't have it any other way. I'm just so happy you're doing well," Uncle Jack said.

I stood. "Unkie, I'm going to put out the last of the cupcakes." I headed to the kitchen for the final tray and moved them to the cooler in the front of the store. I wiped my hands on my apron and took it off. I was feeling a bit fatigued myself. I hadn't done much, but the excitement of the event must've gotten to me. Maybe some fresh air and movement would help.

I returned to the corner, and Taylor rose. "I should head back up front," she said. She jutted her head in the direction of her little art gallery. An elderly couple entered the store. They took one look at Taylor's work and grinned at each other. The woman pointed to the book, *Rejected Drawings*. Throughout the entire night, visitors young and old had all enjoyed her work.

"Til, why don't we take a stroll around? I think we can leave Taylor. She's totally got this in hand. And everyone's here to see her anyway." Uncle Jack sidled up to me.

"That sounds perfect. I could use some fresh air and movement to perk me up," I said. I returned my apron to the kitchen and joined Uncle Jack at the front door.

"We'll be back in a bit," he said to Taylor. She waved as she packaged up a piece the elderly couple had purchased. I bet they would have quite the story to share about it with the visitors to their home.

I tucked my hand inside Unkie's elbow. We turned left from the antique shop toward Florence's. The town council had partnered with the business association to deck out the sidewalk that fronted the ocean-facing shops. Authentic bamboo tiki torches dotted the walkway, the flames brightening the path. The palm trees in the distance swayed with the gentle breeze. The sun had just dipped below the horizon of the ocean, appearing as if it had fallen off the end of the earth. The sky's colors ranged from medium blue near the setting sun to a deep navy overhead. A half-moon shone over the beach, providing a fair amount of light for the nighttime bonfires and the Arts Walk attendees.

We stopped at Florence's window to see the artist she had chosen to partner with. Inside, we saw illustrations that also looked like comics, except the characters in the drawings were Japanese. Uncle Jack and I looked at each other. He raised his eyebrows. I laughed. "Me too. I would have thought Florence's artist would be a painter of eighteenth-century royalty pieces or perhaps a sculptor. But not this." I pointed.

We stepped forward to read the posted bio and artist's statement. McKenna Dalton drew Manga, a style of comics developed in Japan in the late nineteenth century. They were intricate and gorgeous. Nothing there would match the beach-themed decor in my cottage, but I really wanted some of her art. Looking at it inspired me to do even better at my baking. "Let's go in on the way back. I need to have one of them."

"Me too," Uncle Jack said.

We continued our stroll along the sidewalk, away from the antique shop. The Ferris wheel in the distance was lit up like a Christmas tree. Squeals of delight came from the riders every time it took a turn. I looked back over my shoulder toward the location I had seen Poppy's body fall when I sat atop the wheel. It didn't seem the investigation was any further along. I needed to brainstorm with Fiona to see if she had any idea what could have happened. I blinked to get the vision of the body out of my brain.

There seemed to be quite the crowd still, entering shops and enjoying the Arts Walk. I had to give it to Hazel. With the command of a general, she had organized a very successful event. One location that was not getting a lot of love was Poppy's Pizza Parlor. Uncle Jack and I stopped in front and peeked through the window. Not a soul inside, except Dean, seated in a booth, scrolling on his phone. No artist was there either. Was this the end of Poppy's?

I looked at Uncle Jack. "Is there something we can do? It just doesn't seem right that the business would close at no fault of Poppy's or the people that work there."

"Hmmm. You've given me an idea. Hazel won't like it, but I think it's the right thing to do." Uncle Jack continued down the sidewalk.

"OK. You're going to need to give me more than that," I said.

"You are nothing if not naturally curious. Always have been," Uncle Jack said. He pointed to a bench.

I shook my head and we continued down the sidewalk. "This might actually benefit a lot of businesses. But what if we asked people for now to come to Poppy's once a week? At least until her family decides what they're going to do with the place."

I put my arm around Unkie's waist and hugged him. "You are so thoughtful," I said and squeezed him.

"I know it's the same others would do for me. We look out for each other in this town. For better or worse, it is like a family." He stopped and pointed again.

A small musical ensemble located on the boardwalk with a drummer, ukulele, guitar players, and a singer entertained the crowd. A few couples stood on the perimeter of the group, hugging or holding hands.

I looked toward the gathering, my tension releasing even more. What a dream place Belle Harbor had become for me.

Unkie elbowed me and stuck his finger in the direction of the musical group. I followed the angle of his arm. My hand flew to my mouth to muffle a squeal. If it wasn't Barney and Florence holding hands and swaying to the music?

Uncle Jack's eyes sparkled in the moonlight. And I was sure a small part of that was his thought about ribbing his friend Barney about his budding romance with Florence.

The two of them looked into each other's eyes, oblivious to the world around them. Oh, the enchantment of the beach could soften even the gruffest of personalities. I hoped only the best for them.

I tipped my head up toward Uncle Jack. Was he hoping for the same type of relationship? Was it time for a romance in his life? He enjoyed relentlessly kidding his friend, but maybe part of that was a bit of wishful thinking that he had a love in his life. "We should head back," I said.

We turned and retraced our steps back to the antique shop. My head was now clear and my energy had returned.

CHAPTER TWELVE

The cool air from the morning fog washed over my face as I started my run. Today my plan was to pace myself. I wanted to improve my fitness, and running gave me a chance to see a lot of Belle Harbor in a short amount of time. OK, maybe a longer time for now. The light cloud cover would soon burn off, revealing another perfect day at the beach. I knew storms blew in periodically, but we were so lucky here to have near-perfect weather year-round. It was surprising more people hadn't migrated to the small town, but to each his own.

My clip had progressed to a fast walk. My breathing was steady. This was a much better beginning to my run than the other day. I breathed in deeply, hitting a stride for a slow jog. This might just be my canter for quite a while, which was fine by me. The time of day must have been a bit early or the weather a smidge too cool for the morning porch coffee crowd. I looked at my watch to see twenty minutes had passed, and I wasn't ready to quit yet. That was a success in my book.

I slowed as I approached the base of the lighthouse. I had to see for myself the location at the top of the cliff where Poppy had fallen from. I looked up at the railing that had been repaired. The path up was steep, and I wasn't sure I had the proper shoes for that hike. But I had come all this way and wouldn't stop now. The trail had wooden railroad ties as steps every several feet. I pulled myself along using the handrail on the right of the trail. Halfway to the top I looked to my left. The steepness of the terrain kept me from seeing the spot where Poppy had landed. I turned and continued the remainder of the way to the top. The stabbing pain in my side returned times ten. Running on a flat surface was one thing, but add in hills and I was done. I winced as I bent over to ease the pain.

I straightened up and looked down the path to the spot where I guessed Poppy had tumbled from. My heart hurt for her and her family. No matter what happened, nobody deserved to die that way. With the ache subsiding, I moved in that direction. The uneven path was littered by small twigs. I wove around them to avoid tripping. I neared my destination and gazed to my left. The fog hung heavy over the water, stubbornly refusing to yield to the morning sun. I retrieved my phone from my pocket to capture several angles from the scene.

Later I would share them with Fiona so she could help me figure out the scenario where Poppy ended up dead on the sand at the bottom of the cliff.

Losing my balance, I fell sideways into several bushes along the path. I sat for a second, gathering myself. My knee stung with a scrape from hitting a branch. My phone had slipped from my hand and was several feet away in the shrubbery. I stood and parted the bushes, finding it lodged in a mound of dirt. I retrieved it and wiped the grime onto my shirt. It still looked operational. With the uneven ground, I wondered if the same thing had happened to Poppy with her fall. Had she gotten distracted, stepped on something, and lost her balance? I really wanted it to be an unfortunate accident and not a nefarious scheme leading to her death.

I stood and steadied myself, taking a few measured steps out of the brambles, brushing dirt and leaves from my behind. I stepped to the edge of the railing, carefully placing each foot on solid ground. I peered over the edge. It must have been at least a fifty foot drop. Would the fall have killed her? Or was she dead before she went over? From my vantage point I now had more questions than answers. I definitely needed Fiona's help sorting it out.

My hip ached, leaving me with a reminder of my clumsiness. I descended the path for the return trip to my cottage. I hobbled several steps at the bottom and began a slow jog to go home to change.

I turned my thoughts from the tragedy of Poppy to my bakery. My success had become bittersweet as I approached a crossroads from small corner kitchen in the Checkered Past Antiques shop to needing a space of my own. As I jogged by several locations, I tried them on for size in my mind to see if they might be the one. I couldn't see myself in any of them. I definitely needed Unkie's help for this. I returned to my cottage, showered, and changed to start my day. The moped Uncle Jack had purchased for me rarely got used anymore. Only when I had deliveries far enough to warrant revving the thing up. Thankfully, the walk to the antique shop was short and my new endurance served me well.

I rounded the beach and the sidewalk along the shops. Up ahead I spotted Florence shooing what was now two chickens from the front of her store. Apparently the first hen had now brought a friend with her.

I waved and hollered, "Good morning, Florence. I have something for you."

She took her broom and attempted to scoot the chickens from the sidewalk to the sand. She was fighting a losing battle. Those ladies would not be dissuaded from taking up roost in Florence's Bookstore. I am not sure what it was that attracted them specifically to that location, but it did provide some comic relief to watch all parties try to win the war.

I zipped into the antique shop, retrieved the box with the tea set, and placed the batch of crumpets on top. If this didn't soften her rough edges, I was out of ideas. I stepped outside and saw Florence had won the first round. The chickens were off pecking through the sand, possibly finding crumbs from all of the visitors from last night's event. I wondered if those two lived next door to me. But for the life of me I couldn't figure out how or why they came this far.

I followed Florence inside and set the box on the checkout counter. "Uncle Jack and I found this beautiful tea set and thought you might want it for your book club." I removed the crumpet box and set it aside, pulling one of the mustached cups out of the box and handing it to her.

She took it with both hands and gently held the piece, examining it from all sides. She looked up, her facial features softening, and peered over the top of her glasses. "It's beautiful." She set it down and peered into the box. "You have the whole set?"

"Yes. They're yours if you would like them," I said.

We silently unpacked all of the pieces and placed them on the counter. "What's in the box?" Florence asked, pointing to the crumpets. This was the moment of truth. Thankfully she was in favor of the tea set, so I hoped that goodwill would permeate my bakery offering.

"Traditional English crumpets," I said and gulped. I moved the box in front of her. She leaned over and looked through the clear plastic window in the middle of the top. "I hope you like them."

"You made them for me?" She placed her hand on her chest.

I nodded.

"Would you like to have a cup of tea and try them with me?" Florence asked.

My mind exploded. This was far beyond my wildest imagination of responses I expected. *I guess you never know.*

"That would be lovely," I said and followed her back to the corner with the table. Uncle Jack wouldn't believe it. I sat at the table while Florence prepared the teapot. Gwinnie was gently snoring in her bed in the corner. It was rare that she hadn't ventured over to visit Willie. The two of them had become fast friends. Maybe that portended well for my future with Florence. Maybe.

CHAPTER THIRTEEN

I chalked it up as an extremely successful day. Albeit my trip to the park didn't provide me with much more than a skinned knee, a sore hip, and more questions to ponder about Poppy. But my gift delivery to Florence was a huge hit. I hoped that would earn Uncle Jack and I some brownie points for quite a while.

I finished my prep for the next day to make the order for Mocha Joe's. It always helped start my morning on the right foot when I could pull my sleepy self out of bed at o'dark thirty to begin baking if I knew my setup was ready and waiting for me.

"Uncle Jack, why don't I get a pizza from Poppy's and meet at your house?" I asked.

He looked up from his paperwork, his reading glasses perched on his nose. "How about the Dragon?" he asked.

"Um, no. I would like to get some sleep tonight. How about the Quentin Florentino?" I hooked my backpack strap over my shoulder.

"Too many veggies. Chicken Club?" he offered.

I had my phone out, ready to call it in. "Deal. Don't stay too late. I'll head down to Poppy's, then meet you at your house." I figured I would have to wait a bit when I got there since it was such a short walk.

Uncle Jack had been hired to run an estate sale. Normally, customers brought their items to him. He knew his antiques backwards and forwards, but he was spending extra time to make sure the event went well.

I really hoped Uncle Jack's plan for sending people to Poppy's helped them stay in business. I realized I should have ordered a second pizza for leftovers. Maybe I would surprise Unkie with the Dragon after all. He could have it to himself.

The light from inside Poppy's shone through the window. I neared the front door and saw only one customer at a booth. In the food service business you didn't have much of a margin to cover times when business was slow. Was it too late to save the pizza parlor? I pushed open the door to the rush of garlic assaulting my senses. My eyes watered a bit. I sniffed. I looked at my watch to see it had only been five minutes since I had called in the order. I spied through the door to the kitchen that Dean was in the back. He was talking animatedly to Stella, who wore her bright fuchsia lipstick. Her head bobbed as she mirrored Dean's emotions. She stuck her finger in his face.

I wanted no part of whatever that was. Just give me my pizza and I'll be on my way. I chose a seat opposite the lone customer to give him some space to enjoy his meal. The background music that Fiona and I enjoyed on our last visit from the other day was not playing anymore. Other than the occasional fork hitting the plate from the customer, I could faintly hear Dean and Stella. I turned my head and looked at my watch. Any minute now I hoped Dean would appear with the to-go box.

Voices raised louder from the kitchen. "I'm shutting you down. You've had ample opportunity to make a go of this place. I need a business in here that can pay rent," Stella said.

"You can't do that. Just a little more time. And if we don't get it, I'll have to go to your husband," Dean retorted.

"You'll never turn this place around. You're just a mid-thirties loser who couldn't find any other job. Nobody will believe your story anyway," Stella yelled.

I stood to see if I could catch their attention and interrupt. Stella swung her bag, knocking a bottle of olive oil onto the floor and whacking Dean in the head with the purse. Dean bent to pick up the bottle and Stella smacked him again.

"Stop that. I think we can work together if you'll just listen. I knew about the affair between Poppy and your husband." Dean stepped back to avoid another swing of the bag.

"You have sixty seconds to convince me." Stella stepped back and crossed her arms.

"Look, I was blackmailing Poppy about it. I convinced her to teach me everything she knew about the business. She was also giving me a cut of the profit. I knew I was better with the food and better with the finances. My goal all along was to take this place over," Dean pleaded.

The timer sounded for the pizza to be removed from the oven. Without missing a beat, Dean grabbed a large wooden paddle and scooped it out of the oven and into an open box waiting on the side.

"I know that I can make this place highly profitable. And you can get your share," Dean said. He closed the box over the steaming pie. I hoped it was on its way to the front of the store so I could escape this drama.

"You're making good sense. How do I know you're not scamming me just to save your own skin?" Stella sneered.

"You have every right to be skeptical. Give me a month. If you don't start to see it turn around, it's yours. At least with me here you can have a little money coming in while you look for someone else to lease."

They didn't look like they were making a move anytime soon to deliver my pizza. I glanced over at the guy in the lobby. He wiped his mouth with a napkin, pulled out his wallet, and left some bills on the table. He looked at me and shrugged, scooted out of the booth, and left. I was on my own.

"On one condition," Stella said.

Dean picked up the box. At least it seemed he realized he had customers to serve. "What's that?"

"You don't breathe a word of the affair or your blackmailing of Poppy. If that got out, it could look really bad for me in the investigation of her death," Stella said.

"You mean murder," Dean replied. He stared at her. The conversation had taken a dire turn. I needed my pizza and to quickly exit. I moved a step to the side so that Dean might recognize movement through the kitchen door window. But he didn't move an inch. "I won't say anything as long as you keep your end of the bargain."

It was time to take things into my own hands so we could all get on with our lives. I skirted the end of the counter and pushed open the swinging door to the kitchen.

CHAPTER FOURTEEN

S tella took two steps back. "Tilly, you startled me. What are you doing back here?" she asked, looking around the kitchen like I had stepped into a sacred location.

All that I could see were her neon lips moving, the lipstick color prominently displayed. The swinging door slowly settled back into its closed position.

"Well, I came to get a pizza for Uncle Jack and myself. He suggested all of the businesses band together and support Poppy's until the place can get back on its feet." I took a step closer, my phone in my hand, ready to make a call.

Stella hugged her bag, now using it as a shield. Her voice stuttered. "That's a good idea." Stella looked at Dean, her head jutted out. "We all try to stick together in this town, don't we, Dean?"

Dean stepped back.

"Except when we don't," I said. With my free hand, I pulled the lipstick container from my pocket. I held it up to Stella's face. "Are you missing something? This is exactly like the color you wear. And it's one of the high-end brands that you're so hoity toity about."

Stella looked at my outstretched hand and back at me. She reached a hand to her chin. A tear formed at the corner of her right eye.

I glanced at my phone and pushed send to dial the number I had input before I entered the kitchen. "You couldn't take the embarrassment of Poppy having an affair with your husband, so you killed her."

"Where did you get that?" Stella said through gritted teeth. She attempted to swipe the lipstick from my hand.

I quickly dropped it back into my pocket. "You know darn well where I got it." I looked at my phone and saw the call had connected. I only hoped it was Barney on the other end of the line, listening to our conversation. "The top of Belle Harbor park. You must have struggled with Poppy and it fell out of your purse."

"Lots of women wear that color. It could have been anyone," Stella said. She stepped to the side away from the kitchen door leading to the lobby. "Besides, when I left Poppy she was alive."

"So you were there?" I continued.

Dean looked back and forth between Stella and me as if he were watching a tennis match.

"I admit that. But we talked business, then I left. I was having lunch with a friend at the lighthouse. We finished and I saw Poppy outside." Stella slid her left foot closer to the back door. "She was so far behind on her rent, I couldn't let that continue. This is a business, not a charity."

"And you didn't argue about the affair? That your husband was having with Poppy?" I asked. One more piece to the puzzle and the picture would be complete.

"That was nothing but a rumor that nasty people were spreading." Stella shot dagger eyes at Dean—a message to keep his mouth shut or else. He held up both arms in defense. He hadn't made a peep since I stepped into the kitchen. I didn't blame him.

"But it wasn't just a rumor, was it Stella?" My voice softened. I needed to keep her talking for just a few more minutes.

She sniffled and straightened. "You'll never pin anything on me. Finding that lipstick at the park proves nothing. I own this town." She was now only a few steps away from the back door of the kitchen that exited to the alley. If she got that far, she might get away.

Stella raised her voice. "If you and your crazy uncle can't see that by now, you're dumber than a stump." She held out her designer purse. "This place will finally thrive once we can replace some of these dumps"—she looked around and flicked her arm—"with high-end stores. We will become a destination resort for celebrities."

If nothing else, that woman had incredible delusions of grandeur. Enough people in the town wanted to retain the quaint, unique feel. And I had no doubt that would happen.

Just as Stella reached for the door handle, I flipped the pizza box with Unkie's and my dinner into her escape route.

Stella squealed and continued her attempted departure. Her foot landed squarely in the middle of our Chicken Club pizza and she slipped down hard onto the floor.

Dean rushed to the back door, blocking any further attempts by Stella to leave.

Stella sat up with her knees bent, her head buried in her lap, and sobbed. She turned her head to the side and said, "If it weren't for your oily pizza I would have gotten away. No wonder people quit coming here."

I shook my head toward Dean. "Don't listen to her."

"I know," he said. "And Tilly, I think you just earned yourself pizza for life."

Stella tried to right herself and slipped again in the spilled olive oil. She wasn't going anywhere anytime soon. If I hadn't experienced it in real life, the story would have sounded like something out of a cartoon.

Dean kindly grabbed a couple of towels and tossed them toward Stella. For his part in this drama, he would have to live with the guilt of his role in blackmailing Poppy. But her death was all on Stella.

I looked at my phone and saw the call had disconnected. My heart fell. *Barney, I hope with all my being that you heard everything and are on your way.* At least Dean and I were witnesses to the confession. And if needed, maybe Barney could track down the guy in the lobby, if he had heard or seen anything.

"You will regret this. Mark my words," Stella said. She scooted to her knees just as Barney entered the kitchen.

I stepped back. "Please tell me my call went through and you heard what you needed?" I held my hands in front of me, fingers clasped.

Barney looked down at the mess of pizza crust, toppings, oil, and Stella. "It looks like quite the food fight in here," he said.

"Yep. I'm sure Uncle Jack is wondering where in the world I am with dinner. I guess I'll have to come up with plan B," I said.

Barney wove through the puddles of oil and dough and reached to pull Stella up by her arm. He moved her to the counter, turned her around, and grabbed both wrists to lock them into cuffs.

"Tilly, what do you say I make up a couple of pizzas for you to take? Barney, am I allowed to do that?" Dean asked.

"All you want. I got what I came for. Though, after I process Stella, I think I need to come back for dinner myself," Barney said. He firmly grasped Stella's upper arm and guided her around the counter and through the front door.

Stella sniffed and wiped her face on her shoulder, glaring back at Dean, lipstick now smeared around her mouth like clown's makeup.

My hands shook. "I think I'll wait in the lobby and give Uncle Jack a call," I said. Thankfully we now had answers to Poppy's death. I only hoped the pizza parlor carried on in her name.

CHAPTER FIFTEEN

Ruthie guided our group along the wharf toward our party boat for Uncle Jack's birthday bash. "Here you go. Captain Brad will take care of you from here." She gestured toward the vessel that would host us for the next three hours. I had arranged for all of our supplies to be delivered ahead of time. Pizzas from Poppy's, of course. Fiona supplied the ingredients for her classic Paloma cocktails, and the biggest treat of all: my work of art was a three-layer chocolate cake with sweet cream-cheese frosting and multi-colored sprinkles covering every inch.

The majesty of the cake paled compared to what Unkie deserved. It wasn't hyperbole to say he saved my life. The joy I'd discovered since moving to Belle Harbor was far beyond what I ever considered possible. Now, I was learning to live my life on my own terms.

"Thank you," I said, and Ruthie returned to the boat rental office.

The captain guided each of us onto the boat, holding our arms as we boarded. The vessel was a vintage Thomas International school bus converted into a seaworthy boat.

We all took a seat and Captain Brad provided the tour safety instructions. The boat gently swayed, reducing my stress from the previous several days. Tonight was all about celebrating a wonderful man, nothing else.

I opened a box of party supplies and retrieved our hats, the biggest for Unkie. I stretched the elastic and situated the pointy cap on his head, giving him a little peck on the cheek. He grabbed my hand. "Tilly." His voice quavered. "This is wonderful. Thank you."

I smiled. Every bit of planning was worth seeing that smile. I passed party hats around and thankfully there were few groans about putting them on. Unkie and his close friends were in for a night of celebration.

Captain Brad had us slowly following the setting sun toward the horizon. When the daylight dimmed enough, strings of lights lining the perimeter of the bus boat would enhance our party atmosphere.

Fiona opened the other box of supplies for the cocktails and began preparing a couple of pitchers. She handed us each a glass and nodded to me.

I stood. "First of all. To Uncle Jack. Happy birthday and here's to many, many more." I raised my glass. Everyone mimicked and chimed in with "Cheers!" I looked around. "I also want to thank all of you." I took a deep breath, my emotions bubbling at the surface. My voice stuttered. "You've made me feel like this is my home."

Uncle Jack stood and hugged me. "We're lucky to have you. Especially Barney!" Unkie poked at his friend.

"Well, I can't say I wasn't grateful for your help in catching Stella. The use of your phone was brilliant. She's going away for a long time. I'm just sorry for all of the damage she left in her wake. Her husband, Poppy, the pizza parlor ..." Barney's voice trailed off. Florence was seated next to Barney and she put her hand on his arm. They lovingly gazed into each other's eyes.

"How did you know it was her?" Unkie asked and handed his glass to Fiona for a refill.

"Maybe we should get some food going too," I suggested. The boat had a warming oven where we had stored our pizzas. Justin stood and joined me to retrieve a couple of boxes and set them out for serving. I got plates, napkins, and forks from the box and passed them all around. "It was the lipstick I found in the bushes on one of my runs."

The group took turns serving themselves a slice of pie and returning to their seats.

"I had only ever seen one person wearing that. And when we were at the business owners' association meeting, Stella mentioned how her purse had fallen and things had jostled around inside," I said. I grabbed a slice, put it on my plate, and sat.

"You've always been good at connecting dots, Tilly," Uncle Jack said and took a big bite of the Dragon. With the meat and hot peppers on that pizza I just hoped Unkie wasn't up all night with heartburn. "You are one busy lady."

"I love it. The variety of activities helps to keep my brain sharp. Speaking of which, you have a pretty big event coming up," I said. I stretched my legs in front of me, relaxing for the first time in a while. I pulled my toes toward me, my calves still a little tight from my running.

"Yeah, the Wheelers have asked me to run their estate sale. I haven't done that in quite a while. And I'm going to need your help if you can spare any time." Uncle Jack pointed at me.

I laughed. "Maybe we both need to hire assistants."

Barney stood. "Enough of this chit chat. I was promised music and dancing."

Who knew Barney was such a party animal? "You're right. Fiona, would you please get us started?" I asked.

She stood and moved to the console housing the sound system. This boat had everything you could want to make the experience memorable. Fiona started us with the soothing sounds of slack-key guitar music, reminiscent of the Arts Walk.

"May I have this dance?" Barney held his arm out toward Florence. Her smile warmed my heart. She stood, taking Barney's hand and he enveloped her, swaying to the music and the rocking of the boat.

We ate, we danced, we enjoyed the company of friends. I didn't want the night to end. Captain Brad had made the turn at the halfway point, and we were on our way back to shore.

"Everyone, can I have your attention?" I asked. They all took their seats. "Let's sing and eat cake." I gestured to the tall, round sprinkle-covered layers. Barney launched us into the happy birthday song, belting it out for his friend.

I got a knife and sliced the cake, handing the biggest piece to Unkie. I handed him the plate, and he stood, turning to face the group.

"This little lady here"—he paused, gazing into my eyes—"is my gift." He continued looking at me. This was getting sappy, and I hoped I wouldn't lose it. "If I could have designed a daughter from scratch, she would be exactly like you."

I wrinkled my nose. The words were deeply heartfelt, but I was not used to or interested in being the center of attention.

"I am blessed every day to get to spend it with you," Unkie finished.

The group applauded. My face reddened and heated. I had no words. But I would spend every day he had left on this planet showing my gratitude for his generosity of taking me in when I was at the lowest point of my life.

"We're just getting started, girl. This is only the beginning," Uncle Jack finished and grabbed his glass, raising a toast to all aboard.

Are you ready to follow Tilly and Unkie on their next set of adventures? Get books 4 – 6 in the Belle Harbor Cozy Mysteries Collection.

ABOUT THE AUTHOR

Sue Hollowell is a wife and empty nester with a lot of mom left over. Finding a lot of time on her hands, and as a lover of mystery novels, she began telling the story of a character who appeared in her head.

One thing led to another and the Treehouse Hotel Cozy Mystery series was born. Through this experience she has discovered a love of writing stories, and especially mysteries. She hopes you enjoy her books as much as she enjoys writing them.

Sue misses her spaniels that passed, but they live on through her cozy stories. She loves cake, and the more frosting the better!

You can follow her Facebook for the latest news.

Printed in Great Britain
by Amazon